THE
LARK
IN
THE
CLEAR
AIR

THE LARK IN THE CLEAR AIR

DENNIS T. PATRICK SEARS

McClelland and Stewart Limited

ISBN 0-7710-8027-1

McClelland and Stewart Limited
The Canadian Publishers
25 Hollinger Road, Toronto

PRINTED AND BOUND IN CANADA

My father and mother were Irish
And I am Irish too;
I bought a wee fiddle for sixpence
And it is Irish too;
I'm up in the morning early
To greet the dawn of day;
And to the lintwhite's piping
The many's a tune I play. . . .

Joseph Campbell

Dedications, in my opinion, are too often tedious and overly sentimentalized, yet without the inspiration provided by the two most important women in my life: my wife Ellen Morgan Van Pelt and my daughter Mrs. Theresa Aileen Brigid Switzer, this book would probably have remained unwritten. I am also indebted to Robert Anthony O'Brien, Editor of the Editorial Page of the Kingston *Whig-Standard*, for his intellectual assistance over a period of many years.

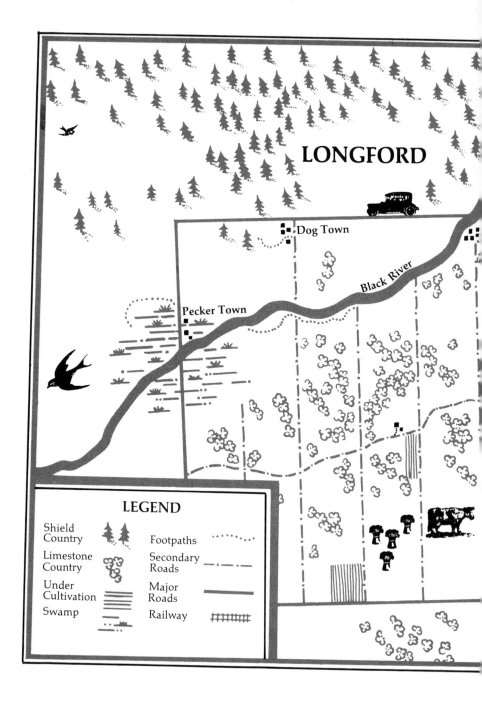

LONGFORD

Dog Town

Black River

Pecker Town

LEGEND

Shield Country	Footpaths	
Limestone Country	Secondary Roads	
Under Cultivation	Major Roads	
Swamp	Railway	

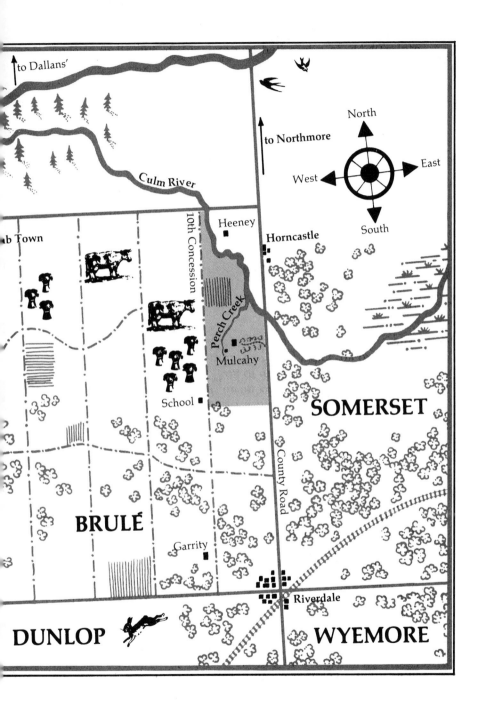

PREFACE

Brulé Township is mythical to the extent that, insofar as I am
aware, no place of that name, township or aught else, exists.
Brulé is a composite of all back-country Ontario farm and town-
lands that have, or had, a marginally agricultural tenure. Many
years ago I heard an elderly country man refer to a burned-over,
uncultivated area as a *"brulé."*

The characters with which I have peopled Brulé, too, are
mythical; any similarities of name or habit to persons living
or dead are purely coincidental. Yet the characters are real
enough to anyone familiar with the time period and the type
of locale. They were not pioneers, but the descendants of
pioneers and the horde of itinerant workmen, many of Irish
birth or extraction, who built the railroads, the canals, worked

in the lumber camps, and stayed to settle these fringes of civilization when the railroads were built, the canals dug, and the lumber felled.

It may be argued, with cause, that any novel is, after a fashion, autobiographical. In that sense the episodic nature of *The Lark In The Clear Air* reflects slices of life as I knew it from that part of my boyhood spent growing up in Ontario.

ONE

If you were of a mind to go looking through old newspaper files of 1931 you would find, along with pictures of the shuffling unemployed, a column or two about the shooting. That's where my story is going to start. It was the shooting that kicked me out of childhood into maturity with no time for any discovery of the sweet youth that should lie between.

I suppose my mother was no better than she ought to have been, but as I see it today, adultery is hardly a killing offence – if it were there wouldn't be enough people left to make the bullets. The law in Alberta frowned on rough-handed personalized justice, too, because after my dad caught mother and her paramour in a situation too flagrant for even a woman's capacity to lie out of, he slammed half a clip of .44.40's into her vital organs and went on the hunt for Jack Sturdivant who had leaped out of the window and into the buffalo brush without his pants.

That brush country of Alberta is tough enough to roam around in wearing boots and a good set of Lee's but, when a couple of hundred pounds of bull Irishman sets to track you down with a Winchester because you stopped over in his bed with his wife an hour longer than discretion dictated, a man needs neither pants nor boots to put miles between the place where he is now and that which he came from.

It must have been quite a chase and in another context it might even have been comical: father was currying out the foothills for Jack Sturdivant, and the mounted police with a string of hounds owned by a half-breed called Wittimack Joe were only a whoop and bellow behind father. I saw no humour in it then and I don't now. One of the mounted had cantered into the school yard where I was playing scrub baseball. He went spur-jangling into the one-roomed school and in a few minutes the teacher came out with her face all peaky and white and wearing that mixed expression of the better class citizen which is a blend of pity for the sorrows and contempt for the hurrahs us brush-popping range-outfits got ourselves into. Anyway, she told me to get right on home without telling me the reason why. She didn't have to; a fifteen-going-on-sixteen-year-old boy raised the way I was raised can presage things. I flipped the saddle on my little mustang mare right in the school stable, and ducking my head under the lintel of the barn door put her on the dead run the three miles to our unpainted frame house.

The mounted policeman tried to catch up but the mare and I knew the road, so he was still a dot of scarlet tunic back on the trail when I slid the mare onto her hind legs and piled off into the house. The doctor was there and a bitter-eyed neighbour woman who had thoughtfully brought along her train-band of snot-nosed kids to show them what the wages of sin amounted to when payday came around.

Mother was dead and had been for an hour. If she said anything worth listening to before she died I never heard about it. She hadn't said anything of any particular interest or value

14

in the thirty-five years of her life so I don't suppose she got any inspirational flashes in her last minutes. Besides, a hatful of slugs from a big rifle hardly sets up the recipient for a round of dialogue.

I had seen shootings before but this was personal. There is a lot of blood from a gunshot wound, and the fellows that write about it or make movies around it never seem to catch on to that fact. There was blood all over the bed; it was splashed on the walls along with last year's fly-dirt, and there was a gummy puddle of it on the floor where mother had rolled off the bed and died.

She may not have been much, even by brush standards, but she was my mother, and I fell on the bed they had hoisted her back on and where she had been entertaining Jack Sturdivant, and bawled my eyes out. I don't know whether I was crying for mother, for dad, or mainly for myself for being caught in a web I never spun.

The doctor patted my shoulder and said, "There, there. Everything's going to be all right." And I wondered what in hell he knew about everything going to be all right – him with his new Model A Ford and his brick house in town and his five-thousand-per whether he earned it or not. The neighbour woman came in, not wanting to miss any juicy details that would set her up as the focal point of the gossip squad at every Ladies' Aid meeting until freeze-up. She insisted that all I needed was something to eat. Had she been right a lot of the world's miseries could be solved: all you have to do after looking at the slaughtered corpse of your mother is to nip out and cook yourself a good rare steak and forget the whole thing. . . .

The next week was a whirl of mist in which events danced round and round in a haze. I can't describe them rightly and I won't try to and I don't want to, anyway. There was a funeral for mother, following which Jack Sturdivant came crawling out of the sage and rocks and knelt in the streets of Stettler and kissed the boots of the first mounted policeman he came to.

Father never came out. Not by his own efforts. He came out of the bush in a wicker basket carried by four sweating half-breeds, and lighter by half of his face and brain-pan that the big, soft-nosed slug had torn off when he tipped the rifle barrel under his jaw and pulled his last trigger. He was forty-five years of age and strong as a bull and as wild as a grizzly. He shouldn't have had to die that way. I think he died when he walked into the bedroom, and his chase after the man that made a cuckold out of him was the spring winding down. The many that liked and admired my father just as cordially detested his wife, and they universally and noisily proclaimed that mother wasn't worth shooting, much less worth father's suicide. That may be. Father was in love with her and that made her something. Then he shot her and that made her nothing. He was a man to the last and threw his own life into the kitty when the hand ran dry.

Jack Sturdivant got clean out of the province and into British Columbia where he worked around logging camps, leaping like a hare every time a bull-cook rattled a pot lid. He became something of a pitiful joke until he died on the streets of Vancouver begging nickels for wine. So he paid a rough price and maybe more than what it was worth, and certainly a lot more than he bargained for. I don't feel sorry for him but I'm not about to judge him, either.

Other than myself, representing all that was registered of father's progeny, get and issue, the only relative to attend the burying was dad's younger brother, Patsy. He was working close enough so that the train fare both ways was negligible. After the solemn rites, muttered with a half-heart by a lazy priest who reckoned he'd be lucky to get the cost of the candles for his trouble, Uncle Patsy and I went out to the cruel little house that still smelled of violence and hatred and smoking death.

"There isn't," said Patsy, eyeing the layout unenthusiastically, "enough here to scratch up a feed for a flock of hens."

He stuck his hands in his pockets and kicked with melancholy at the stove leg. "Besides, there's some talk going around among the holy and nosey that you ought to be chunked into some kind of a home and taught something. I can't take you, and I wouldn't if I could because I think you're going to be bigger than Con and likely just as mean. What you'd better do is light out and I'll tell you where to go."

I was to go, Patsy said, to Victoria County in middle Ontario where I had a great-uncle on my father's side named Mick

Mulcahy. This great-uncle was pushing sixty from the wrong side, lived all alone in a warren of a house built for better times that never came, and was just soft enough in the head that he might take me in, meanness and all. It was either that or get flogged into some sort of government home and have to study the Bible regularly with the risk of being buggerized and sodomited by the kind of hired help provincial authorities took on because they had been scout-masters and cub-leaders and pool-lizards around YMCA's.

In a couple of days Patsy figured out a deal whereby I could get working passage east with a stock-car of halter-broke broncos bound for Toronto in exchange for feeding the horses, sleeping with them at night and sitting up with them during the day to see they didn't kick themselves into the dog-meat they were slated to become after they got there. I could even take my own mare if I wanted, but I sold her for $35.00 to a horse-dealer from north of Thrush and went into Drumheller to see the man who was shipping the horses to Ontario.

His name was Troy Eaton and he was a run-down little cuss of fifty who driddled out a string of blasphemy between bites of Pilot cut-plug. Yes, bigawd, he'd take me on for the trip all right, but by jesus I better see that them sons-of-bitches of bastard horses got fed and I could feed myself in the bargain because he wasn't about to do it, and if I didn't like the set-up there were a thousand men waiting just out of sight behind the bushes to leap up and take on the chore in my place.

Seeing that I was in excellent company, Patsy said good-bye and we shook hands. I was sorry to see him go because, outside of that great-uncle I'd never met, Patsy was the only living relative I had. Fifteen is a lonesome time anyway; here you are with near a man's build and too much of a man's feelings, but you've still got that unlicked touch to you – like a green colt that has never scouted much beyond the palings of the home pasture.

It was beginning to get dusk in the railroad yards. The red and green of the switch-lights began to glow ruby and emerald, and off behind a stalled line of box-cars a switch-engine rammed from reverse into full forward with a spin of the drivers – *CHUFF CHUFF chuff chufffff*. A killdeer ran and cried across the cin-

17

ders, and all the light suddenly went off the rim of the coulee and everything turned blue, then purple and black.

Troy Eaton came wobbling back across the ties with a curious way he had of walking, like a hobbled goat.

"Where'd you get to?" he said irritably, "I been lookin' fer you. My outfit's over here," ducking his head toward some stock cars and a rattly-looking utility car sitting on a neglected siding where the russian-thistle was climbing up all through the ties.

I followed him over and he outlined my chores. "You kin bunk in the cook car with me and Sperl. I was only funnin' you about the grub. I put the grub up, but I can't pay you no wages, so that better be gawd damn well understood. There's three of us – me'n you and Sperl. Sperl's an old feist from a ranch down around Pincher Creek and he's along to go'n see a married daughter of his down in Toronto. He ain't much good and crippled some, so you'll have to lug most of the bastard water for them nags and bust open the bales to feed 'em hay. Once a day you gotta get in the car and dung her out and throw in fresh beddin' on account of them piss-willows of humane inspectors likely to come nosin' around and snoopin' and fartin' and tryin' to tell a man his business.

"Well, come in the cook car. There's blankets there and a bunk fer you. Are you hungry? you can cook your own stuff. I got supplies in and there's ice in the chest. There ain't damn all to do tonight, but I'll be rousin' you out come daylight to water the broncs and dung 'em out an' feed 'em."

The cook car was overheated and stunk for god's sakes of horses and stale feet. There were two bunks at one end and another bunk along the wall. A pot-gutted iron heater crammed to the gullet with Drumheller coal glowed cherry-red. An elderly man in levis and stove-up range-boots was stretched out in the lower end bunk reading a Street & Smith western Romance by the light of a brakie's lantern. Eaton said that this was Sperl and that I was Danny-Boy Mulcahy.

"Danny-Boy, eh?" the old man snorted to himself with a mean chuckle as if that kind of name went along with a choir-boy's snood and a castrato's false-tenor.

I wasn't hungry but I fixed myself a mug of java from a big

18

blue enamel pot that was blowing off steam on the heater. I poured in sugar and clotted milk from a can.

"Mulcahy!" barked Sperl, sitting up as if he just remembered it was Christmas Day, and why didn't somebody tell him. "Wasn't that your folks in that shootin' business up north of Stettler?. . ."

I had my dad's big XL knife out to punch a couple of holes in the milk tin. I turned around slowly and let the lantern light shine from the wicked blade that was five inches of sweet Sheffield.

"Where I was raised folks wait to get married before they start asking personal questions of each other. Now I don't have much god damn intention of marrying you, but if you ever ask me any more questions that your long, un-picked nose should stay clear of, I'm going to take this knife and cut your whang off at the socket and feed it to you bloody-end first."

The old nob reared up and then collapsed with a grunt as if I was too insignificant for a hard-case like him to tie into. But I saw Eaton grinning to himself. I had just made myself a part of the outfit.

In a couple of hours I crawled into the bunk above Sperl and tried to go to sleep. Freight cars were being shunted backward and forth with tremendous crashings and hissings and screechings. Big old mountain engines rumbled down the through lines, *whooooooing, whooooooing* with their great bass whistles ripping holes out of the night. I felt cold and lost and alone.

Old Sperl had doused his lantern and was snoring with a shrill gutter like a shingle-saw slicing knotty cedar. His Ranch Romances was tossed on the floor on top of his evil socks. The funny thing about the old pissmire was that he had been a real cowhand all of his working life and was so busy castrating calves and branding manure-smeared steers that the romance of the thing had eluded him entirely. He had to read pulp fiction to find any beauty in the life he'd always lived, and he believed what he read, although forty years of chousing dogies should have told him better. I don't suppose any woman had ever looked at Sperl except to laugh, and his love life was as vicarious and as spurious as the pulp bosh he waded through trying to get some colour into an existence that was only several shades of unrelieved brown.

The following afternoon our three cars of feed, horses and bunk car were made into a manifest and we creaked out of the yards and swung east. I stood in the door of the bunk car and watched Drumheller and my old life drop back in a mizzle of April rain. The only things that had meant much to me were buried back in the brushy hills. I was glad to get away from a place where the name I carried meant only a wife whoring around and a man who thought with his hands and used a gun to settle his turbulences.

The freight carrying us to Ontario moved only slightly faster than a good man could trot. We stopped at every gopher-hole and water-tank and badger-hill; this gave us a chance to water the horses, and the water had to be cadged by hand in two five-gallon pails and dumped into a cast-iron trough inside the stock car. A dozen horses can drink a lot of water, and nervousness and strangeness had made them thirsty to begin with. One freight car was filled with hay bales which had to be cut open and trundled to the horses and tossed in through the door. I had to do most of the lugging and hauling because Sperl was a hill of rheumatics and bursitis and neuralgia. He set up to watch the door so the nags wouldn't jump out and break for the prairie while I forked in hay by the bale.

Cleaning out the car was the worst because you had to chouse the stock to one end while you shovelled manure out the other. The horses were mountain stock not much out of the bronco stage and they could kick the comb off a setting hen or bite the jewels off a dog-coyote, they were that mean.

We loped and galloped through to Winnipeg which took us all of a week's barging, and there was a three-day layover there before we could get manifested into another train for Toronto. The boss and old Sperl left me to look out for the outfit while they went to look up a whorehouse.

The two old rannigans came whooping and belching back about day-up, drinking from a pint flask and crowing and bragging about the touches they'd cut in Big Sadie's and what the frizzled blonde had said and what the half-squaw had done after they got a snootful of bingo down her adam's-apple.

I was not new to sex and had stopped off on the way home from school a time or two to go berry-picking in the buffalo-willow with girls my own age, but store-bought sex didn't appeal to me then and it doesn't now. I like to see a filly wiggle and bounce as much as the next and more than some, but when you figure that every sigh and gasp and moan is paid for at so much a grunt it takes the fun clean out of it and kills the romance of the thing colder than an eskimo's balls.

Three weeks after we had pulled out of Drumheller, the freight hauled into a hamlet called Beaverton which was on the main line of the Canadian National running between Winnipeg and Toronto. Beaverton was maybe a hundred miles north of Toronto and the closest stop on the line to Great-uncle Mick Mulcahy's, so I jumped ship there.

It was grey, rain-dawn and I stood on the wooden platform of the train station and drew in lungfuls of Ontario air which seemed heavier and sweeter than that of the west. I gaped at the huge elms standing with sodden branches dripping onto bare, ploughed fields and pastures just taking on a slight blush of green against the soddy-brown.

I went inside the station and asked the yawning night-agent the best direction to start off for Brulé township. He said he'd heard of it but had never heard of anybody ever wanting to find it, much less go to it, but if he was me and he was glad he wasn't, he'd take the macadam road for ten miles north and then peter off onto a gravel road that ought to get me within smelling distance of Brulé.

"There ain't," he said, "nothing there but wild steers, beaver hay and bog-men."

I thanked him, cautioned him against poking his nose outside where the temperature was only 50° above and where he might get a whiff of fresh air he was unaccustomed to, and set off at a stride in the yellow-grey morning.

The snows had pretty well all melted and the creeks were foaming as brown as vat-run lager, and red-wing blackbirds were back from the south and setting up shop in every marsh and swale where a cattail could sprout, rooking and cleeing and fighting off interlopers. It seems that male birds can't get a wife unless they own a chunk of space they can lay claim to and roust out land-grabbers. This is called natural selection and works out better for blackbirds than it does men, for a woman will up and leave a brick house and go down the road with Black-Jack Davey who hasn't a chamber pot nor a bed to fit it under. Maybe this is why red-wing blackbirds are as sassy as ever and the human birds get mangier and meaner every generation.

I walked about five miles until a farmer turned out of his lane driving a manure-spreader and rumbled up behind me and invited me to ride. I would have just as soon walked because walking was faster and not nearly as fragrant, but I didn't want to seem churlish and besides, I needed more directions than the station agent had been able or willing to supply.

No, the farmer debated, he'd never heard of a Mick Mulcahy, but his father had. While I was chewing that over he went on to say he would be glad to ask his father but the old gentleman had died eight years before of something that had got into his stomach and balled up in there. Then he swung onto his favourite topic which was manure. Horse manure, I learned, was superior to the cow variety, and pig manure was better still. Sheep droppings were the choice of the lot.

"She's just about the best you can get," the farmer argued. "You can put her around your rose bushes or stick her on your garden or bank up your house with her. I'll take sheep shit any time I can get her."

I don't know what brand he was freighting in the spreader, but whatever it was it was high and had been around longer than merchandise of that class should be to come out comfortable.

We ambled along behind a pair of bay plugs for about three miles, the iron wheels crunching and gridling on the pavement, and in all that time the farmer never asked me once where I came from and what I did while I was there. He talked a blue streak and it was all about manure – the way it used to be, the way it was when he was a boy, and the bad way and state it was in today.

It's an odd thing that a man can live for forty years and know only one thing and have uncertain and likely damn fool ideas about that. He'd been around his cow-flops and horse-balls and pig-pies so long that he'd taken on the appearance of a stack of dung himself, along with the aroma. The skin on his face and hands was a dirty green-brown and he chewed a mean-coloured cut-plug that could have been whacked out of a pile of the stuff he was carting. I wondered too, about a man like that when he got into bed with his wife and what he did to her after he got there. And how any woman whose olfactory organs were not burned out or tied down could stand the touch and sight and stink of a fellow whose feet and thoughts were in a manure pile all of his mortal days.

I said good-bye to the manure-man and struck off down the pike for an hour when I was picked up by a fat drummer who wheezed but said nothing because he was too fat to talk and drive at the same time. He let me out where a gravelled road forked away from the paved. An old wooden sign, that dipped and pointed somewhere to Australia and had been shot through and thither several times by venturesome lads with .22's, advised the world that Brulé township was at hand.

The country changed as quickly as the construction of the road. The flat, fertile fields sporting rich, dark loam were waved away, and limestone ridges cluttered with maple and birch and ash and beech rose in undulating combs, marching straight across the road in places so that part of the time I was walking straight up. I was happy, spotting the different trees and trying to figure them out from old books dad had shown me. Dad had been raised in this very country and he had spent hours drawing me wonderful word pictures of everything that grew and flew and dived and dug, including the human section.

"Beeches, Danny-Boy, are easily identified by the smooth, grey bark. They're artists' trees. I mean by that, beeches look like trees used in illustrations. . . .

"Ironwood seldom grows to a large dimension. The bark is fine and strippy. Ironwood burns green and requires no drying. Our people learned this when they arrived in Brulé from Ireland."

Father had a soft, pleasant voice. He was what people called "a well-spoken man." He had considerable schooling and read a great deal, and he taught me early the love and appreciation of books and ideas I have today. His trouble was that he was a buckaroo at heart and the ideas he discovered in books merely clashed and yeasted with the natural maverickness inside. Father was an anarchist of the draw-down-on-them-and-shoot-them variety and his knowledge and insight of Plato and a natural and logical order only served to needle his conscience when he had gone on some drinking and sky-hooting tangle.

Around noon I met an old woman painstakingly lettering her name on her mailbox. I asked her where I might find my great-uncle.

"That one, is it?" she glared kindly at me over a daub of black paint that had stuck to her nose. "I think I know you. You're a Mulcahy all right. Con's boy, from out west, isn't it? I thought so. I knew your daddy, sure, and the fine strapper he was, when he was about your own heft."

She wiped her hands on a rag. "Now you look tired and hungry. Come on in and I'll fix you a bite. No, don't blarney me, son – I've heard all the Irish blather before and it's long since ceased to charm me. Come away in."

I went in the house with her and she set out cold buttermilk and bran buns warmed toasty in the oven and fried side-meat and fried potatoes and huckleberry jam and crab-apple preserves and a pot of scaldy tea. I ate and she was the first woman I'd talked to and she was as gracious and decent as sixty-five years of hard living would let her be. She had the story out of me and who I was and why I was there in five minutes. I wished I could have buried my head in her lap and cried, but I was six feet tall and weighed 180 pounds and tried to look twenty-one instead of fifteen, so I couldn't, but the misery must have showed on my face.

"Yes," she said softly, "we heard about the trouble out there. I don't know whether it was a wise thing you did in coming here. I suppose you had to go someplace, but old Mike Mulcahy is a very strange man. Of course, all you Mulcahys are strange and wild. Right from old Kerwin on down. Kerwin would be your dad's grandfather; I can just remember him when I was very little. He brought his brood over from Ireland after his wife died over there during the famine times. Well, he was supposed to have met a woman and fallen for her and he made a pile of money gambling around the lumber camps and he bought that place of his and built that big house. Then the woman backed down and things fell through. . . ."

I was grateful for the meal and for the directions the woman provided. I thanked her and left with the feeling, more than ever, of not being too sure of what I'd find at the end of the trail.

TWO

Brulé Township is a rectangle of land about ten miles wide
and six long, with the shorter side running due north and south.
Cutting across the northeast corner of the township is the River
Culm, which rises from God-knows-what and God-knows-where
someplace back on the granite rocks of the Canadian Shield.

Great-uncle Mick Mulcahy had some fifteen hundred acres
on the Tenth Concession of Brulé, the winding twist of the
Culm making a boundary for the northeastern part of his property. In the south, this fifteen hundred acres started off as a
rectangle, then convoluted and narrowed in along the banks
of the river until, if you were to look at it from an aeroplane
and could make out the perimeters, you would see something
in the shape of an old finger-post sign.

A thousand acres of that fifteen hundred was land bought by my great-grandfather Kerwin from land speculators who got it mud-cheap from the timber outfits after they had swarmed over it like a band of harvester ants and picked it clean of every stick and knot of decent lumber. Great-uncle Mick had added another five hundred acres on his own right in later times.

This ancestor of mine, Kerwin, was a queer enough cuss, by all accounts; the oddest of a family where odd-balls were not the exception. He had lost his wife in County Mayo, Ireland, although not in famine days as the good lady who took me in and fed me made out. The Famine was twenty years gone sour in the bowels of Ireland when Kerwin's wife died, and then it wasn't from famine but from something they called the summer-complaint, whatever that was. Kerwin had three children who, in order of birth, were: Rosie, John, and Michael. Rosie was to marry a man from Philadelphia and this man made a fortune but no children. Rosie put on airs and they weren't Irish airs, so a considerable gap existed between her and the Canadian Mulcahys. John was my father's father. He had promise, so 'twas said. The promise was never kept because he didn't live long to work at it. He married young, got a job as boss on a river-drive and drowned when his peavey slipped through the bark on a green log and he dived in the roiling waters head-first.

John Mulcahy left a young widow and two children: both boys and both young, Patsy being but a baby; my father, Con, was two years older. Con was the talented one, the powerful, flamboyant kind. It seemed as though, in creating my father, John Mulcahy had exhausted all of his powers, and that there wasn't enough genetic steam left over to make anything much of Uncle Patsy. Patsy never married; never amounted to much. He didn't do much that was good and almost nothing that was bad. His was the kind of vacant, blue gaze that told of the owner never having two consecutive thoughts about anything. That's as it may be; he didn't wind up with his brain pulped by a bullet, either.

The boys' mother didn't get along too well with old Kerwin. She left the home place and took a series of drab jobs and lived a drab life until she died at the age of thirty-seven. Before that happened my father went back and stayed with his grand-dad Kerwin, maybe picking up too many of the old man's whooping ideas. Patsy stayed with his mother whom he greatly resembled both in matter of looks and lack of spirit. When Kerwin died soon after John's wife, the land and what was on it was left to Michael, my great-uncle Mick.

In the year of which I write, 1931, Great-uncle Mick was sixty-five. He had enjoyed a checkered career without bothering to head for the king-row or worrying much about not getting there. He had worked the lumber camps, visited the cow towns of Alberta and the American west, tried mining, then took over running the home place when Kerwin got too old and stove up to handle the place and young Con at the same time.

When I walked down the long, elm-lined lane that April afternoon, Mick was slouching against a post of the verandah that skirted two sides of the three-storied frame house Kerwin had built for the woman who never set foot in it. That's a story I don't intend to go into right now.

Mick was a bull-necked, grey-eyed old maverick with a combing of grizzled hair escaping from under a slouch hat. He let on not to notice me until I was within ten feet of the verandah.

"Who named you 'Danny-Boy'?" he grunted, his grey look fastened neutrally a mile away where the skyline rolled down and got caught in a belt of hills.

I was tuckered-out tired and cross. I'd been tramping since the light of dawn. Besides, I didn't know who was responsible for naming me. I lowered my war-bag to the ground.

"It wasn't my idea – coming here. Uncle Patsy said to."

My great-uncle got out a package of Tuckett's fine-cut and set about rolling a smoke. "It's the first idea I ever heard of Patsy having. I hope it's his last. I can use some help around here. I'll probably work the ass off you. Come on inside."

That was it. Never a word about the shooting. Not then – not ever. I've met good men before and a few since, but none like Uncle Mick.

This is as good a time as any to get out a description of the Mulcahy mansion and get it over with. Old Kerwin was a bear for privacy and he laid his foundations squarely in the middle of his thousand acres and a good half-mile from the travelled road. To get there you had to turn off and wind along a lane between low hills bristling with pine stumps.

The house was a frame, three-storied affair with enough curlicues and gimcracks and knobs and vanes and spires to keep a team of carpenters with a band-saw going for a month of Sundays. The narrow, drop-siding had once been painted, that once being a power of years ago. There was still more than a trace of the original brown clinging here and there; the rest had turned grey. The plan of the building was a forty-foot square, the first floor having a huge parlour occupying all of one half; the remainder was equally divided between a kitchen and a library. The second floor was given over to four bedrooms which were long out of use. The top storey was a catch-all for junk and debris which was too bad to use and too good to throw out. A full-sized basement completed the layout.

Walking into that house was like taking three steps backward into the last century, except for one thing – Uncle Mick woke up one morning and found a power line catering across the country near his northeast boundary and just across the Culm. He got the Hydro people to run him in a bunch of poles, and he sent to Lindsay and had an electrician come and wire the house. The trouble was, Mick didn't go far enough. He put in one wall plug and one light socket and switch, then called it a day. He couldn't see any sense wiring up a lot of rooms he never set foot in.

For outbuildings there was a huge, draughty barn with a gabled roof, a couple of log buildings, a tool shed, a pump-house, and an outside john the hornets had laid claim to and festooned the pole rafters with hives of all sizes.

There were two fieldstone fireplaces, one in the parlour, the other in the library. Mick never lit a fire in either; he said they were too damned smoky and too god damned much trouble. The only other heat in the place was provided by a mammoth kitchen range that was all iron curlicues which had their interstices plugged up with years of soot and grease. The one bulb of 100 watts hung over the kitchen table where Uncle Mick read his Toronto *Daily Star* that always arrived three days late. There was a radio that had three tubes, two of which seemed to be always burned out, but the third worked well enough to bring in a Toronto station if the wind was from the south.

Mick slept on a leather sofa in the kitchen near the stove. He slept there summer and winter, using an old buffalo-robe for a blanket.

There were more books in the library than I'd ever seen in my life. The shelves ran around three walls and they ran clear to the ceiling. They were filled with books: encyclopedias and doctor books and veterinary books. There were books on trees, on birds, on plants, on every natural thing that swam, flew, crawled or skitted along on crutches. There were histories and geographies and tomes on religion. Each layer of books was covered with another layer of dust.

The first time Mick went to the general store, which was owned and run by a man named Rilance out on the main gravel road a mile and a half north in a little settlement called Horncastle, I laid in an order for supplies. If he was surprised he never let on. When he got back with the team and the democrat, I carried in soap and mops and brooms and pails and I went to work. I worked for a week while my uncle rolled cigarettes and allowed as how I was almost as good around the house as a woman, but not nearly so attractive because my legs were too skinny. He never offered to help. He said, by way of explaining, that once out in Montana when he was down on his luck he had had to take a job as a swamper in a saloon, and the shock of it ruined him against ever going up against a mop for life.

In the midst of my exertions, another old bachelor who had a den in the pine grubbings north of the Culm stumped in for a jaw-wag and a spit at the stove lids. His name was George Heeney and his everyday use of the language was as dirty as the quid he chomped on asleep or awake and spitting.

After we were formally introduced and he squeezed off a streak of tobacco juice that burned and sizzled on the stove, I dug out an empty can that had held axle-grease, and formally requested he spit in that and take caution to empty it and wash it out at the pump-house before he left.

That rocked him.

"I'll be a dirty pile of shit!"

"That you are. You'll be a smaller pile if you ever spit on

30

that stove I've just finished polishing," I advised him, scouring the face of the clock with Bon Ami.

Heeney had a mean pig's eye that never settled longer than the beat of a fly's wing on anything. His eyes got a glint.

"Takin' right over from Mick, here, I see."

"Time somebody was." Mick was suavely polite. "Use the can, George."

I was to learn that when Mick was real calm and polite that that was when he was measuring you for a quick jab on the button. Old George must have learned it long before I did because he never opened his trap on that subject again, and he spit in the axle-grease can like he was born and raised to it.

My great-uncle made his living, and a comfortable one, at raising beef cattle. There were always upwards of a hundred head of prime steers and heifers ranging all over the place. Mick would buy thirty or forty spring calves along about June when they were old enough to hunt graze for themselves, keep them until their third year, then drive them into the stock-pens by the railroad siding at the town of Riverdale, and ship them to Toronto. In the winter, he simply strewed hay around the five-acre lot surrounding the barn and running down to where a little creek called the Perch sallied in and out between the low hills before making off to join the Culm. The beeves ate their fill of hay, tanked up on the icy waters of the Perch, and were as happy as all living creatures that are concerned for the minute that is Now and not for the eons that may be tomorrow. When the blizzards came sailing down from Muskoka, the cattle tailed it for the pine thickets up on the prong of land called the Finger and holed up in the calm below the friendly needles until hunger drove them out. Their hair grew as long and unkempt as a mohair goat's, but they balled up plenty of good, marbled fat beneath it so that in the spring they were as plump as geese.

That ranch was about as pretty a place as a man might wish to see. Although the lumber concerns had gut-stripped most of the pine, they had missed about a hundred acres of it up on the Finger. The remainder of the land was mostly low, rolling hills spreckled with old pine stumps and outcroppings of lime-stone that was packed in shaly ridges under the shallow soil. Several hundred acres were returning to woods: second-growth maple, ash, hickory, hornbeam and beech grew well spaced out and were so cropped underneath by the cattle that it looked like park-land. On top of some of the hills aspen and balm-of-gilead made a crown; down by the Culm, white birch and spruce clustered, and along the Perch there were thickets of alder and pussy-willow.

After I'd been there a couple of weeks and had got dug into the set-up of things, I scrounged out an old sleeping bag of Mick's that he had used for hunting. It was an eiderdown-filled affair with canvas over that and warm enough to sleep you naked at 20° below zero. I took the bag and an India-rubber ground sheet and made a sleeping-out rig for myself down by the creek where the water sang all night long beneath the alders and where the spring peepers were just starting to tune up for the long mating not far ahead. Prior to that I had occupied one of the old bedrooms on the second floor, but the air was musty, and the windows were glued shut with time and old paint and a couple of lifetimes of neglect and disuse.

It turned out to be a good life. Mick was one of those early risers; no matter how quick I turned out of my soogans I would see him up prowling around the cattle corral or striding nice and easy like a mountain man through and around the ridges, smoking his hand-rolled cigarettes. I would take an axe and assault one of the pine stumps until I had an armful of fat splin-ters gleaming with yellow resin. These I laid in the throat of the kitchen range, poured on a dribble of kerosene and touched a match to them, sending billowing snarls of black smoke gutter-ing up the stovepipes. I'd whomp us up a feed of fried eggs and side pork, or flapjacks with new-caught trout I'd relieved from the Culm. My uncle declared I was the best cook he'd ever come across since the time he used to take his meals in a cat-house out in Colorado someplace. He asked me if I'd ever been in that particular cat-house and was it there I'd learnt the profession of chef.

After breakfast Mick would amble away and be gone for hours

leaving me to dust around and flog the dishes. The dog went with him. I haven't mentioned the dog before so I'll do so now. He was nearly all wolf, as silent as a ghost rising out of a grave and pretty nearly as scary. He'd never look you straight-on, but if you turned sharp, you'd catch that big lobo studying you carefully, turning his gaze a shift to fix on something else the minute he figured you were on to him. He never paid me the slightest attention and managed to look through and beyond me, but he never took his eyes off my great-uncle, watching his every move and wag of the jaw. When Mick would get up, the dog would get up. George Heeney told me that one time a two-year-old steer went mad and was set to prod a foot or two of horn into Mick's innards. The dog moved like a beam of light and tore the throat out of that critter with a single snap. His name was Fenris which, I learned from the books in the library, was a name for a wolf. It was a good name and fitted the owner well.

One morning, when the larder had hit low tide and I couldn't find enough Tea-Bisk left to batch together a pan of flapjacks or find a single egg, we scotched along on a breakfast of unmilked tea and a couple of pieces of rat-toast scorched into indigestibility by pronging the bread on the end of the fly swatter and holding it over the pine fire until it had an even coating of soot and cinders on both sides. Although there was a single hen about the place, alternating its roosting habits between the barn, the pump-house and the back-house so as to keep a jump on any night-walking fox, it was in the way of being a pensioner long past the age and urge to lay eggs if it ever had done so.

"You had best," said Mick, "hitch the team and get what you need from Rilance. And you might consider a pair or two of denims and some shirts for yourself. I saw you scrubbing that outfit you got on in the creek, and it's apt to poison the cattle."

The team also classified as pensioners, having been around for much longer than that class of animal can rightly or decently hope for. They were big, old, spraddle-hipped, spavined bays with a lot of Clyde in them because their fetlocks were huge and hairy and looked like hummocks with a coating of dried twitch grass spread over top. The harness was recent and in

33

good condition, oiled and with the bright work seen to and rubbed up so that it glittered in the May sun. The rig was a democrat, which is to say, a sort of light wagon bed and box with buggy wheels and a spring seat up front from where the driving was done. There was a centre pole and king-pin with a doubletree instead of a pair of shalves, and a whipple-tree like you'd find on a regular buggy.

It was a very pleasant trip to Rilance's and the metropolis of Horncastle, although hitching a team like that on a democrat was like coupling a mountain engine on a single mail-car. The plugs had two gaits: one was slow and the other was full stop. The last one they did best as they seemed to have perfected it through a lot of practice.

We crossed a pole bridge over the Perch and sauntered down under a row of elms, the tops of which were noisy with crows and starlings just back from wherever it was they spent the winter. There was a good spring smell in the air; between the hills, the hollows were filled with run-off and melt water that bounced the sky right back at it, and frogs were setting up a living jingle that kept me company almost all the way to the road and the board gate. I turned north on the road, left the new concrete bridge that crossed the Culm, then in rip-roaring flood, and made the straight jog into Horncastle.

Horncastle wasn't much of a shindy then, and I suppose it's less now. The one general store was the only place of business unless you count the blacksmith shop operated by Charlie George when he felt up to it, which wasn't often. You get the notion from reading books that might be thought to know better that all blacksmiths are big, brawny men standing to the forge and letting their muscles swell. Charlie George wasn't enough to fill a middling-sized chamber pot; his wife could lick him the best day he ever lived. On top of that he was sickly and spent his spare hours doctoring and drugging. I don't know which came first, the sickliness or the doctors, but one worked on the other and gave his life a turn of interest it otherwise might not have had and one that he couldn't have got from sharpening ploughshares or beating on horseshoes.

The blacksmith shop was a sorry-looking affair, cunningly constructed so that the rain and wind could get in through one-

34

way holes that didn't let the smoke out. The smithy stood next to a two-storied brick house that was an outstanding monument to general unimaginative Canadian architecture. There Charlie and his wife lived, fought, squabbled and went to bed.

Ed Rilance, his wife, and an unmarried daughter pushing thirty kept the general store and post office. They lived up over the store. Ed wore a collar and tie every day of the week. Now in his sixties, Rilance had a hatful of remembrances and recollections about old times and old timers that leaked all over the place whenever he could buttonhole a wayfarer who would stop long enough to listen. If you wanted to know who used to live on Lot #7 on the 10th Concession of Brulé in 1889, Rilance could tell you. He could tell you what they generally had for breakfast, what their kids died of, and the name of their dog. He collected gossip the way a fly-pad collected flies, although he always got his information second-hand and ready to turn stale.

The only other structure of note in this hive of industry was a patch-and-thatch church that had a tin roof gone to pigeons and rust, and a bell tower with a piece of rotted rope to mark the spot where the bell used to be in better times.

Brulé was a township largely dominated by Irish Catholics, who came from the West of Ireland; that is to say, they were mountainy men – long in the leg and wide in the shoulder. They brought with them, along with their lice, bedbugs and a dash of cholera, their native religion: Roman Catholic. They built a huge brick church in Riverdale and a big brick house as a pasture for the priest. Riverdale was a town about five miles south of Horncastle on the same road; there were about five hundred people living there at the time.

Horncastle squatted on a road which was the dividing line between the townships of Brulé and Somerset, this last being colonized by old Anglo-Saxon stock leaning heavily toward piety and the Revealed Word. The Horncastle church was non-denominational, though it once belonged to the Anglicans who had built it in Riverdale. A bunch of Holy Rollers from Somerset went and hitched a couple spans of oxen to it one cold night and trekked with it clear back to Horncastle where they held a meeting of thanksgiving in it the next Sunday and praised

35

God for his benefices and the fact that the town constable was drunk and sound asleep in his own lockup the night they swiped the thing.

The Holy Rollers rolled out and on and the church was taken over successively by the Plymouth Brethren, the Associated Brotherhood of Apostles, and the Fundamental Baptists of Ontario. In my time there was no regular denomination in charge; any windy devil-chaser with a Bible in one hand and a sermon in the other could come in and announce his presence and call the shebeen to order. He was always certain of getting Mrs. Charlie George and, perhaps, the Rilance girl who, by way of solace for not having fished up a husband, had turned to religion – any religion being suitable.

Rilance never went to church. Skinflint though he was, he occasionally shelled out a few dollars to replace the glass the half-witted Irish boys regularly shot out with .22 rifles. Rilance figured anyone coming to hear a preacher would patronize his store immediately after.

Charlie George was dragooned into going by his wife; he got himself saved three or four times a year, more to keep pace with his wife who went around in a state of grace practically all the time.

Rilance had gone all new-fangled and the McColl-Frontenac Oil Company had put in a gas pump which was a turret-like object with a glass case with the gallons marked on it so you could see how much gas was being used. A hand-lever on the side pumped the gas from a subterranean tank up into the glass tank, on top of which was a white light with the picture of a Red Indian painted on it. It looked nice at night when Rilance had the electric lights on, which was only three days out of the week: Tuesdays, Thursdays and Saturdays when he kept the store open until nine o'clock.

I pulled the rig up in front of Rilance's, climbed off and tied the team to one of the wooden pillars supporting an outside balcony. A woman I took to be the daughter was behind the counter looking out at me across a stack of kerosene cans in the plate glass window.

"You must be the Mulcahy boy we've all been hearing about,"

she said after I'd got through the door and the bell had jangled to announce that someone was there.

She was a well-built girl, a bit on the short side, but with a fresh clear skin. Her black hair was done up in an old-fashioned knot which showed off a trim, white neck. She must have been near-sighted because the glasses she wore were so thick they made her eyes look like patches of brown fog.

I dug a list I'd written up of things I needed out of my shirt pocket, and the girl moved quickly around the store getting the items I ordered from shelves and bins and boxes. I noticed she had good legs; a little thick about the ankles, maybe, but good enough for Horncastle.

While the groceries were being stowed in cardboard boxes, I looked over a pile of men's work clothes and hooked out a couple of pairs of copper-riveted denim pants and two navy blue shirts.

"I guess that's the lot," I said.

"What about drawers?"

That stumped me. I reddened up.

She smiled in a queerly mysterious way and those foggy eyes seemed to swell up until I thought they would come out and stick to the glasses. She trotted down to the end of the counter and came back with a half-dozen of boxer's shorts and stuck them in one of the cartons.

"This will be on Mr. Mulcahy's bill?" She didn't wait for an answer, but went ahead and wrote up the ticket.

She helped me truck the stuff out to the democrat. I was still embarrassed about the shorts and swung myself up into the spring seat and went to drive off without untying the team. That made me look silly. To balance that I swore too loudly. That made me look stupid.

The girl asked me if I ever went to Young People's.

"What's that?"

She said it was a group of young folks anywhere between the ages of twelve and thirty that got together over at the church one evening a week to sing and pray and play crokinole.

"What," I wanted to know, "is crokinole?"

That, she said, was a kind of game you played with round

men like checkers, only heavier. You played it on an eight-sided board that was ringed off in sections and there were pegs and one thing and another to make it complicated.

I was still smarting from the effects of trying to drive the team away with a section of the store tied to them, so I let on I was from tough country and a real bronc straddler from away back.

"The games I'm used to are more interesting," I bragged, realizing the minute I said it I was acting the damned fool.

I got that little quizzical smile again.

"Well, anyway – I'm Doris Rilance. If you would like to come and meet everyone, the next meeting is Tuesday night – eight o'clock."

I said I'd think about it and whacked the plugs across the breeching with the ends of the lines. They were so surprised they almost broke into a brisk walk.

"I think you ought to go," was Uncle Mick's comment when I told him about the invitation to the Young People's.

We were sitting out on the verandah after supper watching a string of Canada geese slide across the apple-green of the sky the sun had vacated not long before. There was a good, rich smell of spring over everything: new-come clover and dandelion flowers and marsh-marigolds as yellow as printed butter down by the Perch.

"I realize you were raised strictly and severely according to the writs and fiats of Mother Church. Just the same – a bit of communion with the King James version and apocalyptic religion may do you some unforeseeable good."

There were times when Mick would shake off his natural Brulé-Irish dialect so that he sounded as if he'd read through all of those books I'd spent the better part of a week relieving of their burden of top soil.

"It will in a pig's ass." I tried to roll a smoke the way I'd seen him do it with a deft, sure flick of the fingers. The tobacco dribbled out one end which looked like a funnel.

"You mustn't use foul language around the horses." The team was cropping at new bunches of clover standing up dark against the lighter green of the yard grass. "They're not used to vulgarisms of that nature. Being of tender sensibilities, your rendering of the vernacular might startle them into throwing a shoe.

"Besides – they haven't recovered from your trying to haul away Rilance's establishment the other day. That particular pair of Arabian beauties have yet to be asked to dray anything heavier than the democrat. It's not fair to ask them to cart off a brick building without first working them gradually up to it."

I was mad enough to throw fits.

"I suppose that blabber-mouthed she-jackass had to tell you all about it."

"You're never referring to the charming Miss Rilance? She has only your interests at heart. She as much as told me so. An ideal companion for you at the Young People's tomorrow night. I've been lying awake nights debating how I might infiltrate you with our local fair sex. This, possibly, is the answer.

"I considered taking you all the way to Lindsay and introducing you to Fat Phyllis, but I doubt you are ready for such a massive undertaking. Youth yet lies heavy behind your unlicked ears."

I was so connipted I went and got my sleeping gear and went to bed down by the creek. Some newly-minted mosquitoes got wind of me and I fought them in a red fury.

While I was trying to doze off I heard Mick strolling softly through the gloam, singing:

> She'll be dancing before you
> Your young heart to gain. . . .

I was set to rise and shy a rock at him, but he crossed the creek on the stepping stones and went off in the night toward where the Culm could be heard roaring and frothing on its far journey to the sea.

THREE

On Tuesday night I put on my new denims and one of the
dark blue shirts and struck for Horncastle. I didn't intend to
let on I was going to go to the meeting. I went into the store
and got a soda pop out of the big wooden cooler and stood
up against the counter a little apart from the others who were
in there listening to Ed Rilance telling about who first built
the log barn back on the Thomas place, where the logs came
from and who cut them and the names of the horses that
swamped them out.

A couple of the group were young, maybe a year or two older
than me, one of them being nearly as hefty, although shorter
and squattier. He kept looking me over pretty good, but I never
let on he was on the same earth. I went and bought a package

of Turret tailor-made cigarettes and I lit one almost like a professional, with a bullet-lighter I'd found in the house.

The Rilance girl came into the store from the upstairs entrance and she made straight for me and took me by the arm.

"Well now, don't you look nice in your new clothes. . . ."

The heavy-set lad snorted and poked the other fellow with his elbow. I cut a mean look in his direction and set him down in my books as being owed something that needed collection before it became a bad debt.

Before anything could come of that, the girl steered me out of the store and we catered across the road and into the church where the meeting was getting under way. There were maybe a dozen mixed gentry on hand milling around beneath a couple of weak light bulbs hanging on electric cords from the ceiling that had big damp places on it from where the tin roof leaked. The whole layout stunk of mouldy hymn books and second-rate sins and third-class sinners.

Doris introduced me around and everybody shook my hand and said they was pleased they was sure, which I wasn't. One real piss-willow of a fellow about nineteen and wearing knee-length bloomer pants made of tweed and checkered socks gave me a real hearty, Christian handshake and said he was real pleased to have me there. He wore gold-rimmed spectacles and his adam's-apple stuck out and bobbed up and down like an orange in a Christmas sock. He was toting a Bible and he asked me if I had found Christ yet. I said I didn't know he was lost and, anyway, I wasn't looking for him.

After more buzzing and scraping, the boy with the Bible, whose name was Wilmot Stroud, got up behind the lectern and said the time had come for all to bow their heads and ask God's blessing on this noble gathering of his young and dedicated. While Wilmot was getting hip-deep into the blessing, one fellow who was closer to thirty than twenty-five reached around the pew and pinched the considerable ass of the girl ahead of him. She just blushed some and prayed a little harder, so I calculated she was used to it and was not a stranger to the wandering finger and thumb.

Somebody got out the crokinole board and four people paired off and started playing. I was asked what I played and I said

41

I liked to play cards. Wilmot said that card-playing was invented by the devil. I asked him who invented crokinole, but he said he didn't know.

Then the pincher came up and started asking me about things out in Alberta – like were the women out there as hot as he'd heard about. I told him a few lies and he topped those, so the time passed until Wilmot came surging out with his good book and started reeling off a few passages about Ur who was known as Sug and what Lem did in the Land of Pashur. The fellow I was talking to, he told me his name was Stew Bodie, sang a little song under his breath just loud enough for Doris Rilance and the pinchy-assed girl to hear.

> Of all the animals in the field
> I'd rather be a boar,
> And every time I mount a sow
> I give her a little more.

With one thing and another the evening trolled on until Wilmot got behind the lectern again and thanked God for allowing us to come in and use his meeting house and if he was willing we'd all be back next week for more prayers and crokinole. And with that the company departed.

Doris and I angled across the road to her place, the lights of which, as well as those in the Charlie George house, were out. Horncastle didn't run much to late hours.

"It's such a lovely night," she said, tucking her hand between my ribs and my elbow. "I'll walk with you as far as the river bridge."

We started pacing slowly down the gravelled road. Overhead the Big Dipper was wheeling slow and timeless; a light breeze from the south stroked our faces and that breeze told of spring coming and marsh-marigolds with their feet in brook water and orioles investigating elms for a likely place to build their queer, cradle nests. Somewhere, out in the black night beyond the rail fences, a woodcock went *"Pee-eint"*, something like a nighthawk, only I knew nighthawks didn't get back from the south that early. A snipe went guttering wind through its feathers away up over our heads.

We walked a half-mile or so and we could hear the rush of the Culm as it tore along in full flood; it sounded something like a freight train on the main line of the Canadian National between Toronto and Winnipeg – the line that crossed the bare swales and granite rocks of Longford twenty or so miles north.

When we got to where we could see the concrete abutments of the Culm bridge, I thought maybe Doris should be turning back; it was a dark night except for the big stars which seemed to be caught in molasses and stuck close to the earth. She said she guessed she'd better, then moved the hand that was on my arm and put her arm around my waist. I may have been a few weeks shy of sixteen, but I'd brushed out with a girl a time or two back in Alberta and I reckoned I knew the signals when I saw them. What I didn't know was how far an older woman would go. I thought to exchange a little light smack on the lips, or maybe two, so I hugged Doris up tight, bent my head to hers and right away I was deeper in the bog than I had calculated on getting. Right then, anyway.

She pulled my head down close, jimmied her knees around my leg so that she had a scissor-hold, and pushed her tongue in and out of my mouth until I had to come up for air. It was so dark her face was only a white blob, but I seemed to see her dark, wet eyes grow larger and larger, only I wasn't looking at her eyes because she had pulled up her dress so that the dead white of her thighs showed like fox-fire against the black of the fence and the shrubbery and the dark, sure rush of the Culm. Even then, being no Don Quilligan, I mightn't have done much except to go off mooning back home to toss away the rest of the night groaning in my sleeping bag, if she hadn't commenced to fumbling with the buttons of my denims.

I had her up against the end of the bridge and she was guiding me to find the place I kept missing, not being equipped with even journeyman's papers for that kind of engineering, yet. As I said, I'd skiddled around with the odd schoolgirl my own age, but this was a grown woman who knew what she wanted and was set to get it. There was as much difference in Doris Rilance and those Alberta schoolgirls as there is between a yearling colt and a four-year-old mare broken to hackamore and saddle and trained to hold tight against a rope dally around the saddle horn when the loop has been tossed over a yearling fetched for branding.

That was the first time I knew of a woman coming to orgasm for which I was responsible, and it came near unnerving me because I wasn't sure whether I was hurting her or if she groaned and carried on that way because she was having fun. And when it was over she turned and ran back in the direction of Horncastle with me looking after her until her white legs got swallowed up in the spring night and the song of the peepers in the ditch-water hid the slap of her feet against the road.

I walked on home without really remembering much about how I got there, my head being in such a whirl and so high in the air and above the mundane things of Brulé it was only a couple of feet lower than the Big Dipper Doris and I had been looking at.

Uncle Mick was still up; the electric bulb was blazing in the kitchen and he was sitting by the stove with his feet up on the reservoir playing his banjo. I knew he'd been drinking because Mick was the best banjo-picker I'd ever heard before or since, but you couldn't ever persuade him to play unless he had several drams of white-wheat whiskey which he said lubricated his finger joints considerable. None of the Mulcahys other than Mick could play so much as a musical comb, so I expect he got it from his long-dead mother who was said to have had musical talents.

So I came in, stepping pretty high and feeling downright superior. Mick inclined his head in my direction and double-picked a real lonesome strain while fiddling with the tension of the strings in a manner I never saw any banjo-picker ever do until the time of Earl Scruggs. He laid his head back and, grinning a little the way he did when something was tickling him, he baritoned out a ditty for my benefit . . .

> Oh, he laid her down gently
> And lifted her clothes;
> And what he done to her
> Oh Christ only knows. . . .

"Have a drink," he said, indicating the jug. "And button up

44

your fly, you've got pecker tracks all over your new pants. It's a very bad example for Fenris, here, who is a very moral dog."

I let on I had to go into the library after something, so I went in there and did my buttons up in a seething fury. I went out and poured myself a good tumblerful of whiskey.

"I'll admit," Mick went on strumming, "you've got something. Usually Doris waits until she's known a fellow at least a week, but in your case she had you out for a midnight ramble among the muskrats in half that time."

"Ha. You don't know so much! That's a girl that wouldn't go out with just anybody."

"You're right there. It would have to be a man – one with lead in his pencil."

I'd been caught out to look bad and I didn't like it. "She said I was the first," I lied angrily.

"True. The first tonight and, with any luck, possibly the last if she doesn't meet a likely candidate on the way home. Where'd she take you? out in Foley's pasture?"

I could see he had me boxed and wired, so I sat and glowered and said nothing that would let him get his needle in farther than he already had it. Mick went on to tell me about Doris Rilance. She mightn't have been a nymphomaniac, but she had the hottest pants north of Lindsay. She wasn't a bad girl and probably would have made somebody a good wife, but seeing as how everybody between the ages of sixteen and sixty had straddled her at one time or another, most bachelors were afraid of hitching up with her for fear of being snickered at. And those that might have been able to put up with the horse-laughing were afraid that if they married her they'd have to chain her to the bed-post or lock her up in the root cellar if they left the premises any longer than it would take to get a drink of water, in case she'd be on her back with her legs up and someone in between them by the time they got back.

FOUR

The next morning I was awakened by the meadowlarks. Every fence post on the far side of the creek seemed to have a big yellow-breasted lark doing sentinel duty from the top of it. I leaned back in my sleeping bag and enjoyed the serenading until a hatful of blackflies found my scent and set to work to make nests inside my ears.

I got up and jumped into my pants, catching sight of Uncle Mick sitting on the log bridge which had been thrown across the Perch to accommodate a wagon trail. The May sun which was rising from behind a bridal veil of mists lying in the direction of Horncastle bounced shards of light off the forty-ounce bottle of whiskey occupying the curb-log alongside Mick. I knew he was off on one of his ambulatory drunks that could last anywhere from three days to three weeks. I hadn't lived with him long enough yet to experience the last and longer variety, but I'd heard about them from Ed Rilance. There was no doubt, declared Ed, that Mick Mulcahy could tote around a considerable swashing of booze, although Tim Connolly, who had first settled around these parts in 1859, or was it 1860? – had held out drunk for nearly two months which was, as far as he knew, an untopped record that took in Brulé, Somerset, Dunlop and Wyemore Townships.

I went and kneeled down by the creek where Mick and the bottle were keeping company, and soused my head a few times under the current. I hoped Mick would not allude further to the previous evening's experience, although I needn't have worried; my uncle had a finely-honed sensitivity where it concerned the fitness of things; once a joke was driven home and reamed around, that joke was over as far as Mick was concerned. Besides, he was always too busy laying out the header furrows for the next one to waste time spudding in a picked-over dry hole.

We sat in the morning's sun, watching the dace flit-tail through the amber water where the green shoots of flags were spearing up as if a whole regiment of one of Pharaoh's hosts were standing to arms under water with the business end of their frog-stickers just clearing the current. For upwards of an hour Mick reached into that pack-rat's nest of a mind he carried around with him, dredging up and trotting out all manner of esoteric information that was a heterogeneous collection of zoology, biology and crapology which was part guesswork, part sound information. He knew, for instance, what made cock meadowlarks sing and fly in the clear air of the day, and it wasn't simply to amuse a half-drunk old man and a raw slug of a youth. They did that, Mick said, for the purpose of staking claim to whatever territory they required to feed themselves and the family they expected. He said it wasn't any different from what the human species set out to do, only a lark knew when to quit and he didn't horn in and fence off a whole lot more land than what he could properly handle or what was needed for any given season. A human had more wart-hog in him than he had meadowlark and that was what was wrong with the world. Mick failed to mention what he was doing by his ownsome with a thousand acres of rambling real estate when two or three might have served him nigh on as well. But then, like all of us, my uncle could see precisely what was wrong with the universe and those that populated it without divining too clearly what was wrong with himself and his own hold on things.

While we were sitting there discussing the habits of our feathered friends, a new model Chevrolet sedan came crawling and bumping down the trail from the direction of the main road. It stopped at the east gate and three men got out. Two were in brown uniforms with peaked caps and Sam Browne belts; the third had on an old felt hat and a pair of bib overalls around which was slung a leather cinch supporting a holster and pistol.

I was wrong about Uncle Mick: he discovered a new twist to an old gag.

"It seems the Rilance girl has laid an information with the constabulary charging you with indecent assault with intent to go only halfway." He laid his eye to the bottle, gauged the remainder, and dolloped it down.

The cops picked their way through the cow puddles and horse doodles to where Mick was having breakfast. The one in overalls was Brad-Awl Callum, weed inspector, pound-keeper, truant officer and County Constable all rolled into one six-foot-four, one-hundred-and-ninety-pound package and armed with a .38 Colt's, the cylinder of which was rusted so tight it might as well have been welded. He was around my uncle's years or a shade nigher the cradle, and Mick had two grudges against him. One was that he was an Orange-Lodge Scotchman; the second was that Brad-Awl was one of the few men in the old days who had been able to stand toe-to-heel with him and trade punches on an even-up basis.

He was called Brad-Awl because he was raised to the trade of harness-maker, but with horses going out of style Callum had to scout around and whistle up a more regular line of work. He had fought with the Canadian contingent during the Boer War and always wore his battle ribbons pinned to the front of his overalls. Brad-Awl looked more the fool than he actually was; he had great knotty hands with sandy hair growing all over the backs, and when he got a grip on something with those hands he held to it like a bulldog with lockjaw. There was a run-down jail with attached office in Riverdale from which precincts Brad-Awl maintained the peace and quiet without ever using his gun because of not knowing how to shoot it if he had to. His main staff of office consisted of a lead sap that must have weighed two pounds, one side of which had a flat run to it from where Brad-Awl demolished Pat Quinny when that misguided fellow rammed a shotgun in the constable's belly.

Brad-Awl had absolutely no sense of humour; neither did he have any imagination, and it was this that made him a first-rate policeman. He never wasted time romancing about things or setting out to figure out ungodly reasons why people broke the law, let their stock bust loose, or failed to cut the tares and chaff along their roadsides. Lacking imagination, he also lacked fear.

My uncle launched himself into a long-winded and sardonic greeting, the sheer beauty of which was lost completely on the trio of lawmen.

"Gentlemen! gentlemen! . . . How delightful, on this pearly morn of May to see the minions of the Law up and about the great affairs of state.

"Danny," turning to me, "do we not all sleep sounder in our beds knowing that at the slightest hint of danger Brad-Awl and his cohorts will spring between us and all harm, interposing the dauntless shield of authority between ourselves and those that prowl by night seeking to do us wrong?"

Brad-Awl took all this in sternly without flickering a whisker. "Hae ye seen Toot Finnerty about in yer pearly May's morn?" he demanded.

Mick admitted that he had not and went on to say that he had been deprived of the sight and smell of Toot Finnerty since late last fall and, with any luck, this deficiency would continue until the coming fall.

I was to learn that Toot Finnerty was a denizen of Slab Town, one of three deserted and half-deserted used-to-be hamlets and lumber centres bunched up about three miles apart over in the northwest corner of Brulé hard against the Longford line. These towns were, in order of importance, industry and total population: Slab Town, Dog Town and Pecker Town.

49

Beginning with the last and least, Pecker Town was so named because in the early days when the lumber concerns were swathing through the stands of clear white pine and driving the logs down the Black River, that body of water lying north and west of the Culm and also being wider, deeper and more anxious to drown anybody that ventured out on it, Pecker Town was a social centre of straddling houses, saloons and boarding establishments that managed to combine the choicer elements of each. The pine was long gone, and the lumber outfits with it. The whores and saloon-keepers didn't hang around to complain to the Chamber of Commerce about attracting new industry; they packed up their various frills and bottles and moved off to wherever it is such concerns go when the spring winds down and the machinery stops. The place was a rook-a-raw of caved-in buildings without a single habitant save a few black bears that were old enough to remember and still prowled the dump in the hopes someone had come back and thrown out a few savouries that made easier pickings than a bear could rightfully aspire to catch on the fly.

Dog Town got its name from there being three times as many dogs whelping round loose than there were citizens. What people there were ran mostly to half-breed, quarter-breed and other fractions of Indians who didn't like being tethered to the government reserve forty miles north under the paternal but constraining eye of the Federal Bureau of Indian Affairs.

Slab Town also harked back to the days of the timbering concerns and the name fitted. It was a collection of shanties made of mill-ends and side-slabs and rough quarterings of pine that even the tight-assed mill owners considered too lean to whack up and ship to Toronto aboard flat cars. The original dwellers, all of whom worked in the camps or around the sawmill, had moved on and dispersed to be supplanted by an even meaner, ornerier procession of troglodytes and chronic misfits, mostly of the order of sub-Irish. The rents were cheap, game was plentiful, and forage such as raspberries and blackberries and saskatoon berries and wild squaw apples could be had for the exertion of arming yourself with a pail and taking your chances of not coming jaw-on up against an ugly bear with the same notions. A wind-washed signpost announced, as if it was hard not to notice, that you were entering Slab Town. On the reverse side some up-country humourist had inscribed the information that you were now leaving Slab Town.

In one of these shacks lived an outfit that my uncle would call a trois-menage; in simpler terms it was Toot Finnerty, his cousin Oliver O'Kane, and a limbersome string of a woman answering to the name of Tanglefoot. They survived by dint of making moonshine whiskey cut with bluestone, scratching up enough ground to seed in a few hills of potatoes, and cutting cordwood from second-growth hardwood in the winter. Tanglefoot was married to neither but slept with both on alternate nights except when drunk, when she slept with both of them. All three had lived upwards of thirty-five years without gathering any more around them than what they stood up in plus a cookstove that smoked and an out-house that leaked.

What brought the full weight and force and majesty of Brad-Awl & Co. down on their unlaundered heads turned out to be a row over whose turn it was to share the ticking with Tanglefoot. Ordinarily, she would have solved the whole business by giving them equal time, dividing herself into two parts with the boundary line drawn up roughly around her belly-button and letting them draw straws to see who would get what half. Somehow, the woman must have been feeling nippier than usual, or else to pass the time she thought a little territorial struggle would proclaim her true worth and to the victor go the spoils. . . . Whatever, the row and the ruction did, as the song goes, begin, and ended with Toot whanging his cousin over the head with a cant-hook, leaving him flat and pale on the floor, drawing a painful breath at the rate of once every two minutes. Tanglefoot ran screeching into the spring airs and collared somebody sober enough to crank up an old flat-bed White truck that had hard, tubeless tires all round, on which they stacked the unconscious O'Kane and galloped to Riverdale where there was a veterinary who delivered calves and babies with equal skill and dexterity. The truck ride over those melting, corduroy roads would have shaken up a hale person into a siege of St. Vitus Dance; for a man precariously close to death it was a hair too much. The veterinary, a fat man by the name of Gower, took a look, pried an eyelid up with two fingers and

51

let it pop shut again. He declared that Oliver was far beyond the prevails of even his incredible feats of medicine and that the only thing left was to take the shabby remains and deposit them with Charlie Bass who was the undertaker and furniture dealer, and who had a model-train layout down in his basement with the tracks laid so that the engines and rolling stock wound in and around the rough-boxes and pine caskets, sitting up on saw-trestles just waiting for someone to come along and lay claim to them.

So the same sun which Mick and I enjoyed seeing shine on the riffles and arrow-heads of the currently water saw fat Amos Gower trundling over to Brad-Awl's three-roomed cottage beside the jail, there to lay the whole thing in the lap of constituted authority who hadn't finished his breakfast yet and solemnly chewed his oatmeal and dug away at the toasted corpse of six-day-old bread while he listened and planned the necessary action.

The first thing Brad-Awl did was to crank up the wall-phone and get Gertie over at Central to connect him with Provincial Police down at Lindsay. What was mere common assault with a fractious instrument and calling for no more than a five-dollar fine and a night in the quod, had turned out to be a first-rate, Grade A case of homicide, for no matter what Oliver O'Kane might be in the eyes of his neighbours, the Law figured him to be a man the same as anyone else, and whoever did him in stood in the shadow of the gallows until the rights and whys of the case got looked into and ironed out.

The Provincial Police, being outlanders to the district and only quartered where the government saw fit to station them, rarely put in their oar around the peripheries of civilization unless acutely required. Mostly they busied themselves with highway traffic or an occasional raid on a bootlegger and moonshiner. Otherwise, keeping the peace fell to the County Constables – men appointed for brawn, knowledge of that and those falling within their bailiwick, plus an ability to brown-nose up to whatever MLA happened to be representing the County at Toronto.

The three constables, driving in the Provincial Police Chevvy, got to Slab Town a half-hour after Tanglefoot, bereaved in one case but anxious to retain a hold in the other, had returned with the bad news. Toot Finnerty wasted no time on solemn good-byes; he made a dead set north for the Longford Rocks where a lone man on foot was as inconspicuous as fly-shit in black pepper and just as hard to spot.

Brad-Awl thereupon cantered over to Uncle Mick's, knowing that Mick was very conversant with the rolling granite ridges, beaver meadows and oak-scrub thickets that made up the scenery of that part of the great Canadian Shield.

Mick was half-pleased; he regretted that his drunk was spoiled, although that was balanced by the pleasure of hunting down Finnerty, for whom Mick had developed a dislike – not on moral counts so much as aesthetic. He got to his feet without so much as a wobble.

"We'll need dogs, so that means we'll need Tom the Indian. And we'll take Danny here, along; if we corner Toot and need reinforcements or a stretcher to carry out some policeman he shoots, Danny'll be handy to send back the word with."

The pair of Provincials paled a little and fingered the flaps on their holsters. Brad-Awl looked scornful. "I aye checked with yon wumman and he's nae taken the auld rifle. He couldna hit a bull in the arse with a handful of gravel, annyhoo. Ye ken thot well, Mulcahy."

Mick grinned cheerfully and we all got in the car and bounced our way to Dog Town where Tom the Indian, his part-time wife, nine kids and a dozen hounds occupied a building that had once been a two-storied hotel and saloon. Tom was sitting on the steps of the sagging verandah, peeling the bark from rods of whistle-willow which his wife steeped for a week in its own broth, added handfuls of this and chunks of that, then sold it as a sure-fire cure-all for anything bothersome from hang-nails to galloping syphilis.

The dogs and the kids all came charging and whooping out of the house to greet the unaccustomed sight of a new automobile. Tom's wife stayed inside the fort, peeking out from behind a set of drab curtains the original owner hadn't considered were worth removing when he packed stakes and shifted on. The kids clustered around the car, leaving smeary hand-prints on the headlights and poking their noses up the exhaust pipe to see where the stink was coming from. One little girl of about four, shyer than the others, hung back and chewed on a piece of hen-dirt.

The Indian had a hundred reasons why he couldn't assemble his dogs and go off trailing Toot Finnerty, and every reason was sound and freighted with unassailable logic. The excuses melted away under the sun of a promise that the County would pay any reasonable fee to dog and man.

Six humans and an equal number of dogs constitutes a fair cargo for any automobile of that day or this. The dogs kept crawling around and over us and one got sick and brought up a lot of steaming offal all over the shiny brown suit of a Provincial policeman. Added to the general uproar was the voice of Brad-Awl instructing the two cops what they might expect once they hit the rocks. If that wasn't enough, Mick had brought along a bottle which he was busy getting the contents of down Tom the Indian. After the first belt Tom began to smile. At the second he began to sing.

> O, he ripped and he tore,
> He cursed and he swore
> And he wiped his ass
> On the knob of the door.

Caravan and cargo arrived at the purlieus of Slab Town where it drew up grandly before the Finnerty-O'Kane demesne, where the several bodies – constabular and canine – burst out and set about whatever business interested them the most. For the Provincial Police that meant finding a place to have a leak at the rear of Finnerty's hurrah's nest. For the dogs it was an opportunity to light into the mongrel population of Slab Town, which they proceeded to do. The battle raged through, in, out and around the shanties, with stray dogs, hearing the foofuraw, coming for miles to enlist with joy.

Brad-Awl, Mick and I stepped through a doorway, the door of which was sagging on leather hinges tacked to the jamb with roofing nails. Tanglefoot was inside holding forth to a few gawping neighbours, giving them the precise particulars of who stood where, who hit whom, acting the whole business out in running pantomime.

Tanglefoot wasn't much, even by Slab Town standards. She could have been twenty or sixty; in fact she was thirty-nine. She was tall and scrawny with a bosom like a mocker-nut shell – it may have swelled up at one time, but there was nothing substantial inside or out that would make it grow or make a woman out of its owner. Her hair had been set upon by assorted dyes and chemicals until it was the hue of an iodined dog. The beginnings of a thyroid condition added a goitre to a long-unwashed neck. Her eyes were pale blue, without feeling and apparently without pupils. They were wild, feral eyes.

No, Tanglefoot allowed in reply to Brad-Awl's none-too-tender questioning, she didn't know where Toot went. The last she saw of him he was crossing what was left of the old mill-dam. He crossed the river and disappeared into the granite hummocks and the huckleberry bushes.

Brad-Awl borrowed an old shirt of Finnerty's and we went outside to give the hounds the scent. The dogs were bleeding pretty lively, having run into sterner opposition than they had concluded on, but they rallied around and got Finnerty's smell, which shows you dogs can stomach a lot more than most humans. They started belling and ki-yopping down the road and over the dam that spanned the Black River, with the rest of the posse bringing up the drag.

Once into the Shield country the hounds ran freely and were soon out of sight. The Provincials dropped behind soon enough; they were neither in condition nor dressed for rousting around in country that several glaciers and ice ages had pawed over in the last hundred thousand years. Brad-Awl asked Uncle Mick where he would head for if he was law-dodging in this kind of terrain.

"The Notches. There's a bit of a cave there and a spring of water. You'll find your boy there, all right."

The Notches was a place where the granite had been all stacked up and tumbled together like a bird's nest made out of red rocks. That place was about a couple of miles due north of the river and the hounds were already there by the time we arrived. They raised their muzzles and wahooed about a hole little bigger around than a coyote den. Brad-Awl forged ahead, peered into the hole and waved us on with a hand as big as a picnic ham.

"Toot! are ye there, mon? If ye're yon, come oot. Hush yer bluidy dogs, Tom, fer the luv' o' jesus!

"Toot! come oot or I'll hae to gang in and drag yer carcass oot and feed it to Tom's hoonds, here."

The Provincial cops steamed up, out of breath and sorts in equal amounts. They wanted to know why they couldn't just shoot the son-of-a-bitch right there and save the County the price of a rope, but Brad-Awl waved them back, cocking his ear to the cave entrance.

"Whut ye say, Toot? Naw, yer wumman nae spilled the beans. ...Ye hae to crawl oot o' there and be arrested so we can hae supper and quit this fashin' aroond."

If you were raised in the west the way I was and had flushed gophers out of their holes by flooding the den with water, you would have an idea what Toot Finnerty looked like when he crawled out, all wet and muddy, from the cave in the Notches. I felt sorry for him. I remembered only too well another time and another place where dogs and men were set to track a man down. I looked at Uncle Mick to see if he was remembering, but he had his half-drunk, sardonic face on. There was a cold glitter to his eyes. I think he was enjoying the whole ramshackle chase; he had no liking for either the law as represented by Brad-Awl or for the wretched, half-drowned caricature of a human being that bellied his way out of a stinking, water-filled hole to the feet of his captors. There was a mean, Mulcahy streak in my uncle that tended to unravel much that was good and warm about him. I wouldn't call it sadism because he didn't thrive on torturing anything; but if he got a down on anyone there was no hell too hot he wouldn't consign that person to.

Toot was short for Tutankhamen. When Finnerty was born, his mother, following the Catholic habit of naming children after saints, looked up in an encyclopedia and found Tutankhamen which she took to be some old mystic Church Father long dead and martyred by the Romans. She must have been bone ignorant, but hardly more so than the priest who baptized the

56

squalling infant Tutankhamen Finnerty. That cognomen was far too big a mouthful for anyone in Brulé to pronounce, never mind spell; it became Toot and the owner lived and died with it, and if he had a headstone, which he hasn't, it would have been carved on it.

To the Toot Finnertys of this world life can appear to set up downright unreasonable. The government, the law, or anyone else or anything else of the whole aggregate of state machinery had never, during the whole of his existence, turned a wheel to benefit Finnerty. Yet here was gathered the full force and majesty of the law – pistols, handcuffs, dogs and Sam Browne belts – gathered together in one place to make a set at him and drag him away to the county seat and maybe hang him for nothing more than what well could be considered a private quarrel involving no one except Toot, the late departed and, maybe, Tanglefoot. If anybody had first claim to being sore and requiring an inch of Toot's greasy scalp it should have been O'Kane, but he was dead and laid out on two planks in the middle of Charlie Bass's rolling stock between a couple of switches and a level crossing. Tanglefoot could make out a case for a grudge: with one stroke of a cant-hook she'd been deprived of a spare bed-partner who could possibly be relied upon when Toot was out of commission, out of sorts, or out of favour.

He crawled out and stood up, all damp and slimy from the interior of the cave, and he looked around at every face and he couldn't have seen much that would raise the hair of a hope. Brad-Awl was reaching for his handcuffs with the stern face of a Scottish Sphinx that has joined the police force; the two Provincials stared at him as if he was some sort of grubby badger dug out from under a hen roost after slaughtering a half-dozen prime layers. Uncle Mick had a twisty, sidelong grin – the grin of a man who is about to slide a foot of bowie knife into you after he's disarmed you and you have no place to run. Tom the Indian, who but for the grace of God and the lack of informers, might well have been rooted out of the same hole, managed to look off-handed, but if the County had offered pay for it Tom would have set his dogs on his own mother and used her hide for glove leather after they caught up with her.

I was stone-cold neutral, which was maybe the worst of all. A man caught up in the thorny side of the law can endure the gibes and the catcalls, but it must be hard to go to the gallows or a prison cell with nothing but a row of aloof, uninterested faces for a mental picture to accompany you.

By the time we all got back to Slab Town the sun had dropped far enough so that the oak thickets, turning pretty with brandnew yellow and green leaves the size of a squirrel's ear, were throwing long shadows across the rocks. The Black River was a steady, sullen roar; the current would dash at the remains of the dam and spillway, throwing up a lather of spray when it hit the rotting timbers.

A crowd was waiting, speculating, pondering and I-told-you-so-ing in the way of crowds and people to whom nothing much ever happens and when something does, everyone turns out to be a first-rate expert who knew it was going to happen all the time and was just waiting for the event to prove them right. Among the gathering were some newspaper fellows with a tripod and a camera. The Provincial Police came to life and grabbed the handcuffed Finnerty, one on each side, and stood up and looked strong and majestic and fearsome – like a big game hunter that has just shot the man-eating leopard and is having his picture taken with one foot on the bloody corpse.

Brad-Awl collared Tanglefoot, taking her along as a piece of live evidence, and the three cops, Toot, and Tanglefoot stowed themselves in the police car and dusted south toward Lindsay. Mick and I were obliged to hoof across country five miles to home. I was feeling good and disgusted.

"I don't know what you're grinning about. . . . That wasn't Legs Diamond we ran down and holed."

My uncle stopped for wind at a snake-rail fence. He leaned heavily on the top rail and I saw all at once that he was showing his years. The booze had run out of him and the years crept back to take its place. Where there had been hard, brown tan there was now a papery grey the colour of a hornet's nest. He took off his hat and wiped his finger around the inside band to remove the sweat.

"No," he said, "that was no Legs Diamond. But he may be

the closest thing to Legs Diamond Brulé will be privileged to find in its midst. We have to make the best of what we can get, considering the distance Brulé is from New York and Chicago and other centres of bandit culture."

His eyes were ice-blue.

"Toot has been guilty of running a shandy or two on me in the past. He is too insignificant for a bullet, and a man doesn't demean himself by batting the ears back of scum like Finnerty. The time was bound to come sooner or later when Toot's luck would drain out and I wanted him to know that I was there to help pull the plug. The intelligence will get around. Brulé has more Finnertys. They will hear of this little disservice I handed Toot and they will know that old Mick Mulcahy has a card or two he can still put on the table to call in the pot."

Out of the sunset a chill wind sprang up, rattling through the still-bare branches of some stag-horn sumacs as we passed. I shivered and felt geese walking over my grave.

FIVE

By that May of 1931, the economic condition known as the Great Depression had every city, town, community and gopher-hole in North America in its toils. This phenomenon has been chronicled by better historians than I, so I mention it only in passing. The Depression hardly fazed me – I'd never known anything other than hard times. Nor did rough scrabbling impose other than normal conditions on Brulé Township. In Brulé, as in many another rural area, a handful of people had the land and money sewed up; the rest hung on and lived by the little that leaked out of the bag. That's one view. . . .

Brulé, topographically, is a terrain of rolling land with a thin skin of top soil stretched to the breaking point by layers of shale and limestone. In many places the shale surged through the soil to lie flat and bare, with here and there a brushy covering of prickly ash that managed to get a root-hold in the crannies and cracks made in the limestone by the action of water and frost. If the geology books in old Kerwin's collection were right, this shale rock was mud from old seas that once covered this part of the earth. I often came across fossils of fish-like things and fern patterns embedded in the naked rock. Once, to my uncle's wry amusement, I set about removing a chunk of rock with a hammer and cold-chisel. I lugged the rock, in which was set the petrified frame of what appeared to be a giant centipede, into the house and set it on the kitchen table where, by the light of the single bulb, I examined the thing and compared it to drawings in the geology books. It took me the better part of half an hour to figure out the stony skeleton was a trilobite and likely several millions of years old.

Apart from long-dead trilobites, Brulé hosted a myriad of potholes the size of sloughs or horse ponds. These water holes were spring-fed; some dried up in the summer, some didn't. Every pond was fringed around with cat-tail and burr reed. Some even boasted a muskrat lodge made of mud and dried bulrushes. Mallards nested there as thick as botflies around a horse's nose, so that every autumn when the season opened the pop-pop of hunters' shotguns sounded like the siege of Verdun.

For the rest of it, the township was covered with second-growth maple, ash, hornbeam and oak. In places these hardwoods grew closely enough to form a wood; in other places they were spread out so that, where the soil was deep enough, a carpet of grass stretched between the trees so that it resembled acres and acres of rolling park. Some of this land had been worked over by homesteaders who had grubbed between the stumps and boulders, sticking in a hill of potatoes here and a handful of seed oats there. Approached that way, the earth wouldn't have supported a pismire, but left alone to lapse back into grass and regenerate, it made the sweetest graze for beef cattle east of the foot hill country.

Brulé, compared to more fertile sections of the county, developed late – if it could be said to have developed at all.

At one time – back in the 1850's – the township was covered with white pine and was owned outright by the Crown. The lumbering concerns made political deals with the politicians and swarmed through Brulé and her sister townships like termites, felling and cutting everything from one-hundred-and-fifty-foot monarchs to sapling-size bean poles. When the snow was deep the loggers cut high on the stump – as much as four feet above ground level. They set up their mills close to their logging operations, floating the sawn lumber down to the rail points. When they had finished, the cut-over areas were less than scenic; piles of tindery brush lay around hundreds of acres of ugly stumps. Every so often, in dry spells, flash fires would roll through this slash, destroying every living thing, animal or vegetable, in its passing.

When the lumber companies pulled stakes, speculators bought what was left for a song and dance. This they, in turn, unloaded onto the gullible, land-hungry Irish who had helped lay the rails, saw down the pine, and dig the canal that lay to the south and was supposed to connect the Georgian Bay with Lake Ontario so that prairie wheat stored at the Lakehead could be shipped with reduced mileage to the cities of the East. It may have been a good plan except that the canal couldn't handle anything bigger than a vessel with a six-foot draught. Even a prairie farmer knows you can't haul much wheat in a ship that size.

So Brulé didn't get settled until the 1850's and '60's. Those West-of-Ireland people who did settle there, one might have thought, had had enough of rock, peat-bog and barren diggings. Maybe Brulé reminded the homesick Celts of the country they had worked so hard to escape; at any rate, they paid ten times what the land was worth and twenty times as much as they could hope to get for it when they sold out and moved on, as three-quarters of them finally did. Only the graziers, who had enough savvy to go into the cattle business, prospered. As they prospered, they increased their holdings by putting the squeeze on the less successful and then buying them out for fare money to Sudbury and Saginaw, Michigan, and Brandon and Regina. Some left their bones in the two cemeteries – the big one at Riverdale near the Catholic church; a little one, now no longer in use, over at Slab Town.

The north-south road connecting Horncastle with Riverdale was the east boundary of Brulé. Riverdale was astraddle a branch line of the Canadian National, the end of the line being some fifty miles up country; the other end tethered into the main line at Beaverton where I had said good-bye to the carload of broncos. A mixed freight and passenger train chuffed up this line once a day and returned the next day. It hauled crushed stone, ties, logs, cattle, and whatever goods and supplies the merchants needed.

Riverdale actually squatted on the intersection of four townships – Wyemore, Dunlop, Somerset and Brulé. Several square miles of this southeasterly portion of Brulé was given over to peat bogs lying continually under an inch of water and covered with a whisker-like growth of low-growing blueberry bushes. This type of terrain, being too thick to drink and too thin to plough, was left severely alone with one exception, when a fellow named McIllheny set up a rig for processing the peat into fertilizer.

For all of his 1500 acres and rambly old house, Uncle Mick was hardly one of the bloated plutocrats the labour journals made out everyone who owned more than the boots he stood up in to be. Beeves were not fetching a top price on the Toronto market and buyers could be almighty choosey. Old Kerwin may have made a little money in his time, but he wasn't the one to save up and lay by simply to allow his descendants to have a life of ease and plenty. My uncle may have had a little to his account in the Riverdale bank; like most Mulcahys, he hadn't the ability to squeeze a nickel until the beaver hollered. He didn't seem inclined to pay me regular wages and I didn't ask for any. When I wanted something, which wasn't often, Mick would toss me five or ten dollars which was more money than I was likely to see around home in Alberta in the course of a year.

Life settled down and bid fair to being pretty enjoyable. We got up when we felt like it, worked when it was necessary, doing a bit today and saving a lot for tomorrow. Beef cattle have a way of looking after themselves, so, except for castrating bull calves and inoculating the entire herd against a stock disease known as "black leg", we had little to do as far as the beeves were concerned.

Mick allowed, seeing as he had young, willing help, that this might be a good time to tackle repairs to the outbuildings, some of which hadn't felt the caress of a hammer since the time they were built. The great barn, a huge building with a gambrel roof, stood four-square and sturdy to any weather; the rest of the outbuildings were beginning to show their age. There was a small log barn – the first barn my great-grandfather erected when he settled in Brulé. This building stood gutted and empty; in the daylight you could see sun stars twinkling through the ragged cedar shingles. The log affair had once been used as a sheep shelter by Mick when, one year, he set up as sheep-fancier. Mick didn't care for sheep; they stank, had ticks, and blatted too much. Mick sold his little flock at something less than profit and spent that on whiskey which he drank while solemnly thanking his own wisdom. On warm days the log barn still reeked of that oily mutton smell peculiar to sheep, and bits of wool could be seen on the pine logs where slivers had hooked them away from their owner.

A framed driving shed, a pump house and an outdoor privy made up the rest of the outbuildings. They all could have used the attentions of a handy carpenter.

Somewhere along the line my father had picked up the trade of cabinet maker and carpenter. Being the kind of man he was, father turned out excellent work and then refused to make his living at it. In Alberta, he was forever putting in a set of kitchen cupboards or hanging a door or setting steps to a front porch for our neighbours. This was work on the free gratis. If my father ever made a dime out of his skill with woodworking tools I never heard of it. When he was in the humour, father showed me how to hone a chisel until it would razor the hair from a shin bone. He taught me how to file a saw, and I ruined no more than two or three hand saws before I acquired the knack of it.

I pestered Mick into letting me have a whack at rehabilitating the buildings.

"You may begin with the backhouse. I believe it was here before father. I think the Indians built it. It looks like something an Indian would build. In fact, you might demolish the existing structure and begin afresh. Take the wagon to Riverdale and get what's necessary at McCandy's mill. I presume you will require tools. Try the hardware store, but don't let Ed Rilance catch you buying tools in Riverdale; he has a few archaeological specimens for sale and he might be annoyed to find I was taking my custom to the city.

"I'll make out a cheque, and with the balance I suggest you buy a safety razor – I notice three whiskers on your chin, just two less than Mrs. Charlie George. Now unless you wish to sing, go and crawl into your sleeping bag – I am about to play the banjo."

While I was setting about laying the keel for a new toilet, I had time to think of Doris Rilance. I knew I had taken the girl by storm and I was conscious of my obligations. Nevertheless, Doris was far too old for me to consider marriage; I schemed of ways to let her down gently.

When I next saw Doris after that frog-filled night at the Culm bridge, she was chatting with a tobacco drummer whose Model A Ford was perched out in front. When anyone opened the front door something like a cow-bell jangled. When I went in the store the bell jangled, but neither Doris nor the salesman turned around.

I cleared my throat to let Doris know I was there. She looked at me impatiently.

"Just a minute, if you please. I have business with the gentleman."

While I cooled my heels, Doris leaned over the counter on which the drummer was lounging so that he got a clear view down the front of her low-necked sweater. I decided there was nothing in the store I wanted to buy. They didn't see me leave.

I was digging a privy hole when the truck came. I had chosen a new site – under an apple tree that was just now budding into blossom. Honey bees, from some apiary, moved about the pink tips making a pleasant humming. A female bluebird investigated a hole in one of the upper limbs. I had dug down to about six feet below ground level so that my eyes were even with the toes of Uncle Mick's boots. He was in one of his homily-spinning moods.

"Let the urbanite," he preached, throwing wide his arms dramatically, "have his cramped cubby beneath the garret. We shall crap 'midst pastoral beauty – 'midst hum of bees and twitter of birds. Our thoughts shall be great thoughts. Our thoughts will be not at all on Doris Rilance who, I understand, attended a box social in Riverdale night before last with a travelling man. Rumour has it he bought her box – figuratively that is. . . .

"Oh, how merry pipes the meadowlark this morning! Have you heard the larks, Danny – from the depths of your turd-grave?"

I hoisted myself out of the hole. "If you're trying to get my goat, don't bother. This hole should be deep enough – even for you."

A red half-ton truck was grinding up the ranch trail; it stopped outside the house and the driver cranked his horn loudly. We walked over and the driver climbed out with a bill in his hand.

"Jesus old ring-tailed Christ! I had a hard time finding this place. I got a bench saw here for Daniel Mulcahy." He pronounced it "Mulky."

"This young man with the shovel is Daniel 'Mulky.' He will assume charge of the bench saw." Mick strolled toward the barn, rolling a cigarette.

"I don't know anything about a saw. . . ."

"You don't have to know anythin' about the god damn thing. Just sign for it. Right there where it says 'Received one bench saw with extension cord and six blades, 10".' Jesus – these roads's awful."

The machine in the back of the truck was pure, shining steel beauty.

The driver, a few years older than myself, pulled a flat packet of Player's Medium from a shirt pocket. He made an impressive ritual out of wetting one end, tapping it on his thumb nail and sticking it in his mouth. He lit the cigarette with a wind-proof lighter.

"Well – where do you want it put? Where'd that old fucker that was here, go? This thing's heavier'n a bastard."

66

"I guess we ought to put it some place close to the electric."
I was a bit dazed with the glory of a machined steel table in
which was set a hungry-looking circular saw blade with great
hooked teeth.

"Well, Jesus Christ – yes! you can't plug it into a cow's arse
and expect it to run. Have you got 220 in or 110? She'll run
on 110 but 220's better. Got any water fit to drink around here?"

While I was trying to pretend I knew what 110 and 220 was
all along, I remembered that the driving shed had wiring in
it, although it seemed never to have been used. The driver
whirled the truck around, backed up with a professional skid
of the wheels, and with an amount of grunting and god damning
we unloaded the machine and set it firmly at home in the driving
shed.

Then I remembered to ask where the saw came from.

"From Manfred Minnow's Hardware, that's where it came
from. Had to send clear to the De Walt people to order it fer
you. I thought you bought the fuckin' thing. I don't work fer
Minnow, jus' deliver sometimes. That's some outfit. Never delivered one like that around here before; she's better'n the one
McCandy's got. There you are – paid and delivered. . . ."

He let out his clutch and roared back up the trail.

I walked around the saw as if it were a holy altar. A brown
envelope tied to the frame contained a book of instructions.
I sat on the tongue of an old hay mower and read the instructions.

There was a hand-wheel to raise and lower the blade; another
wheel tilted the blade over a full 60°. There was a steel fence
that moved smoothly across the table so that ripping cuts of
any width could be made. A cross-cutting guide that could be
angled to every degree of the compass slid like oiled clockwork
in a groove in the table.

By sundown I had figured out a lot I could do with the bench
saw and I had the walls and roof rafters cut out in my mind
and nailed in place. When I bought the lumber from Jimmy
McCandy's sawmill, his foreman, learning that I was merely
setting about to build a privy, tried to palm off some tired-looking
tamarack scantlings that must have been warping quietly around
the lumber yard for twenty years.

"Plenty good for a shit-house."

I bought white cedar two-by-fours, spruce tongue-and-grooved one-inch boards for sheathing, and wide pine siding for the exterior.

"Here's a fellow figurin' to spend a lot of time in the crapper," the foreman grinned when McCandy came out of his little office, thumbs stuck behind his wide braces.

The mill owner looked me over with a quick, shrewd eye.

"That's a fellow that knows good lumber. Who'd you say you were? Mick Mulcahy's nephew . . . *mmmm hmmmm.* What's old Mick up to these days? Don't see him around too much. How many beeves is he running this summer? You want to pay cash? A charge is ok with me. Listen – you want top lumber you come and talk to me. Mick ever tell you me and him worked in the shanties together one winter? Up in Michigan – Copper Country – Calumet. Yessir."

When I had hooked up the saw and turned on the switch, the circular blade spun with a low, deadly humming. Almost timidly, I placed a two-by-four against the guide and fed it into the saw so as to square one end. The blade whined and a stream of white and brick-red cedar sawdust spurted ten feet to the rear of the machine. I examined the cut end of the scantling; it was as square and smooth as if it had been planed.

All afternoon I sawed and fitted and hammered. I sweated and enjoyed the feel of sawdust mingling with good working sweat. I enjoyed the feel of a sharp blade slicing like a razor through fragrant lumber. I felt that the world was a good place and I wished it could go on forever.

Around dusk Mick came back; he said he'd been up to visit George Heeney. He seemed only casually interested in the new saw and the work I had turned out with it. He said that he had bought it to take my mind off women and that my nightmares about girls, down in my sleeping bag by the creek, had the habit of startling him in the middle of the night. If he approved or disapproved of my framing he never said.

"It must be spring," Mick remarked. "George swept out his shack. He does that once every year when he is sure the snow won't return and set his labours to naught."

SIX

Late in May, I noticed a third horse had joined Mick's team of farm plugs cropping negligently in the south pasture flanking the barn. The stranger was a fine little sorrel mare with a good bone structure and a streak of Arabian in her someplace.

"Oh her!" Mick volunteered by way of explanation. "Belongs to Lasher – the horse-trader at Hartwell.

"He knew I had a little extra pasture this summer and asked me to let her run until fall. Kind of a saddle critter – doesn't seem to fit well as a driver and she's a mite light for the plough.

"You might, if you care to, try her in the saddle – an old Alberta cowpoke like you should have no problem. If Gertie doesn't buck you off in a patch of bull thistle you could ride around the fences once a week and help take the daily tally of the cattle beasts – that is if you haven't more interesting outhouses to design. Mrs. Pat Larkin was inquiring of you the other day. Said she'd like that wigwam of hers replaced if you had the time."

The new privy, gleaming and satiny in bright unpainted pine, raised its gabled roof under the white shower of apple blossoms. A pair of barn swallows with sunset breasts were already fashioning a mud home under the eaves.

"If you were to go into the barn and scout the third bin of the granary you would find a stock saddle. The old man must have bought it at some auction years ago. Probably needs a pound of saddle-soap and a rivet or two around the cinch and the stirrups."

The mare, Gertie, was indeed a saddle pony. She reminded me, sadly enough, of my own little mare I had sold before coming east.

Fifteen hundred acres has a considerable circumference. All of this land, except where the buildings were located and the adjoining horse pasture, stood open and unenclosed save for the perimeter of fencing around the outer boundaries. From east to west my uncle's ranch extended from the Riverdale road to the 10th Concession of Brulé – a distance of one mile. From north to south the range occupied more than two square miles, the north end being irregularly bounded by the Culm and the south by another holding owned by the Kelly brothers. Some of the outer fencing was of the old rail-type; some of newer Paige-wire with wood or iron posts. When you have about six miles of fence you have six thousand temptations for restless cattle.

A two- or three-year-old steer is a funny beast. He is neither as dumb as you might think nor as smart as you might wish for. You could take a small herd of this class of animal and set them down on the bald prairie with never a fence or ditch within five hundred miles and they wouldn't be satisfied unless they could find a way to get to Vancouver. With a piece of ground the size of Mick's ranch, covered with sweet lime grass, speckled with water holes where the springs fed clear, cold water to drink all year 'round, and with swamps and boggy places where stock could flee from the heat and flies, you might reasonably conclude that here was Cow Heaven for any one hundred cattle beasts this side of the Toronto Stockyards. Yet a steer would leave knee-high graze to walk over to the line fence fronting on the 10th Concession road just to stick his head through a gap in the rails so he could chew on the Queen Anne's lace and Devil's paint-brush that grew along the roadsides. One out of ten tries and that steer would get his head caught. Then by levering his five hundred pounds in the right direction he could slam down a panel of rail fence or tear the staples out of a post to which was attached a wire section. When that happened, the unreformed bastard would set up a beller and a blat until the rest of his clan had gathered to explore the new gap and set off down the road on wonderful adventures and likely as not to wind up in some farmer's yard where the week's washing was hung out to catch the sun and wind. Fifty or sixty overgrown bovines can make a wonderful hash out of a woman's pants and petticoats or her husband's winter flannels.

Mick was in the habit of walking the fences, spring, summer and fall, but he was getting creaky around the kneecaps for all of his soft way of walking, which was more or less his way of concealing the bursitis inflaming his joints. By the time Gertie and I had made our first lap of the perimeters, I figured out that my riding fence had been Mick's aim all the time. He was cagey as an old he-crow and the more I saw of him and the longer I lived with him the more I came to wonder about this boozey old bachelor living away off in the bull's-eye of nowhere.

Riding along the 10th Concession, I had to pass the school house which was located across the road. There was a yard with a couple of swings made from steel cables and a run-down teeter-totter and the rough layout of a ball diamond. The yard was fenced off from the surrounding pastures; a rim of box-elder and chokecherry bushes followed the fence.

The school itself wasn't much; but then, neither was the student body. The kids came mostly from Dog Town and Slab Town, and no matter what the Township gathered from the parents by way of fines it failed to balance up the loss in back taxes. The building was a one-room affair topped by a slatternly belfry without a bell. It was covered with imitation-brick siding that was peeling at the corners and shedding on the sides. A double john and woodshed combined completed the roster.

Riding near the school one day along about the hour of noon and feeling good at having my boots shoved into stirrups again, I saw the kids out for dinner, eating their jam sandwiches in the shade of the box-elders or wrestling and running around the yard. A couple of the older boys yelled and waved at me. I stopped the mare.

The kids that had waved came across the road and started talking to me. I cocked a shin up on the saddle horn and rolled a cigarette. I felt fairly grown-up and superior – the kind of superiority a mounted man has over a man on foot. Some other boys and one or two girls came over and joined the first bunch. I let them pet the mare and she put her nose over the fence and allowed them to rub her nose, although she turned down the offer of a tomato sandwich one of the girls held out.

The teacher came out on the rickety front porch, shading her eyes against the sun and looking to see what new devilment her charges had let themselves in for now. I could see she was a young girl, maybe eighteen or twenty; young and pretty. She was wearing a dress the pattern and style of which might make its appearance in Riverdale by 1938.

The teacher tripped down the steps, showing a good flash of silk stockings, and cantered across the road. When she came up I saw she was even prettier than I thought. She was tall. I'm crowding past the six-foot marker, but she was mighty near my height was I standing alongside her instead of perched up on the horse like William S. Hart. Her hair was a kind of chestnut flavour, with little gold and red glints. Her eyes were very direct and the colour of willow-water in June when the new bulrushes and pickerel-weed are just poking up through and turning the whole pool a shade that isn't either blue or green or brown but a soft jumble of all three.

"I hope the children aren't bothering you," her voice was as soft and round as flute notes.

I flicked my hand to the brim of my uncle's cast-away hat.

I wished that I had gone to Riverdale for a real haircut at a barbershop instead of letting Charlie George whack off the surplus with his hand-turned horse clippers.

"That's a very beautiful animal. . . . And you ride beautifully. I've seen you once or twice. . . . You sit a horse like a true westerner. Are you from the West by any chance?"

I admitted to my origins, grinning with pleasure at the compliments, somehow forgetting that when I smiled, my teeth, crooked and uneven from a kid's accident, were not the kind that flash at you from an Ipana toothpaste ad. I closed my lips quickly.

"You taught here long?"

"This is my first year – also my first school. It – it's not at all how I imagined my first teaching position to be. Have you been in the East for some time?"

"Coupla months."

"Oh, then we're both practically newcomers," she laughed and it was water falling gently over rounded stones.

I leaned forward, idly scratching under Gertie's mane. There was a touch of fragrance in the air different to that of the chokecherry blossoms – a hint of something foreign and exotic: jasmine or sandalwood like they sell in city drug stores. Through the teacher's thin blouse I could see the white impress of her brassiere and the soft swelling – like May-apples – behind that again. I felt the blood seeping up my neck, so I turned away and concentrated on scrubbing away at the horse's neck.

The girl glanced at a wrist-watch encircling a slender arm delicately veined. "Goodness! it's nearly one. Ta ta, I hope to see you again when you pass by. Wave if you see me, won't you?"

And she was off across the road, shooing scampering kids ahead of her while I watched the pleasant jouncing of her fanny.

That evening Mick and I sat out on the verandah with our feet on the railing. The sun was dropping behind the elms and sending trailers of shadow out from every tree and bush. A night-hawk beeped high and out of sight, then dropped with a purring of wings. Mick ran his fingers across his banjo strings, touched the right chord and began to sing softly to the coming night.

> The girls of Cork City
> They're fine and they're grand. . . .

He had a pleasing voice. Not professional maybe, not the way you heard some sing on the Grand Old Opery on Saturday nights, but it was a nice easy baritone you could sit and listen to all night without getting tired. The songs he sang were country, Irish, and sometimes a popular air. Some of his songs I'd heard before and some I hadn't and haven't heard since. I wish now, looking back, I'd written the words down or studied harder at catching the tunes.

"I guess I better hitch the team tomorrow and haul some rails over to the 10th fence. There's a place there big enough to haul a load of hay through.

"Ridin' by the school today. . . . Talkin' to the school teacher, Miss what's-her-name. . . ."

"I wondered when you would be meeting Miss Warren. Alas, I have sighted her only rarely and that from a distance. I do not like to go near a school. It saddens me to see the boys imprisoned. But word has reached me that the 10th has a jewel. Did you know that I am a trustee? I read Miss Warren's letter of application and approved it on sight. A most beautiful hand: clear, poised, yet slanted enough to be interesting.

"The last teacher left hurriedly. One of the Slab Town lads crept up to her desk and squirted turpentine with a water pistol up her leg."

"I would hate to have to teach a gang of hogs like that."

"Yes, no doubt. But even hogs are required by law to have some acquaintance with the tools of learning. Young Ryan tried the turpentine trick with Miss Warren. She crowned him with a world globe. I believe Dr. Gort inserted several stitches. Yes, Miss Warren may do well."

The sun was well down behind a dark, cigar-shaped cloud; the night-hawk had been joined by several others; their low thrumming when they plummeted down to snatch a winged

74

insect was a sweet, gentle sound – like a low note of Uncle Mick's banjo. It felt good to sit on the verandah in the apple-green gloaming, hearing the bawl of a distant steer, the easy run of Perch Creek among the sweet flags and watercress, and thinking about Miss Warren – the school teacher. I wondered if she liked to go walking in the May dusk under wild crab trees all bridal veiled in creamy blossoms – whether she liked to sit on a rough pole bridge, listening to the gurgle and suck of creek water on its way to the salted ocean – if she liked to stand beneath an elm shaped like a vase and watch a female oriole threading bark stringers to make a hanging nest.

About that time Mick bought an automobile. He got it second hand from the Chrysler-Plymouth agency in Riverdale. It was a 1928 Plymouth – the first Plymouth the Chrysler people brought out; it had four cylinders, hydraulic brakes, and its four doors made it a sedan. The paint job was a robin's egg blue.

I hadn't even known Mick could drive a car.

We cleared the long unused implements out of the driving shed and stored the Plymouth in there. Mick taught me to drive, gigging backward and forth across a hard, level strip of pasture until I could shift gears and let the clutch out with a minimum of grinding. Mick was not a patient teacher, but then I was not exactly a quick learner. Once, in disgust, he drove the car back to the shed, swearing he could teach George Heeney to be a chambermaid quicker than he could show me the rudiments of steering, clutching and braking. Inside of a week, and with the help of Mick's sarcasms, I could pilot the Plymouth along the Riverdale road without lurching from ditch to ditch. I became a competent driver and maybe even a safe driver without becoming really good, and I am not a good driver to this day.

Mick was conducting a lesson with me on the 10th road late in the afternoon when we overtook Miss Warren, arms filled with books, walking south from the school to her boarding place with the Garritys.

We stopped, and Mick was out of the car and holding the rear door open with one huge hand while lifting his hat with the other. The sun flashed on the silver waves of his hair, and his strong white teeth with the two gold caps made me conscious of my own malformed set. I began to realize that my uncle was an extremely handsome man. The realization sent a dart of jealousy through my liver.

"Do get in, Miss Warren. How providential! I've been intending to call on you. I'm Michael Mulcahy, one of the trustees. You will recognize my nephew – Danny – a Chevalier Bayard without his horse."

The teacher climbed gracefully into the car, favouring Mick with a gleaming smile that had so charmed me a week earlier and infuriated me now. I managed to let the clutch out too fast so that the Plymouth jerked and growled and then died completely. I ground the starter button in a fury and we dusted down the road.

"So you're the very mysterious Mr. Mulcahy I've heard so much about. I knew you were on the School Board, but do you never attend meetings?"

"I prefer to send my opinions by mail. Besides, the chairman – old Garrity – who doubles as your landlord, was named to that high office over my emphatic objections – I felt that chairmen of school boards ought to be able to read and write. I understand Garrity's wife has to sign his X for him."

Miss Warren giggled.

"Nevertheless, Aughrim – as the Irish say – is not lost. Which brings me to the point of my wishing to call on you: through a bit of arm-twisting I have convinced the Board to supply two hundred new books to the existing miserable library in the 10th School.

"The Board had its own ideas about titles and content, but I have recommended your complete jurisdiction in the matter of selection. You will, perhaps, be gracious enough to arrange a list of titles for me and I will manage delivery within – shall we say two weeks?"

"But Mr. Mulcahy – I – I'm overwhelmed!"

She remained overwhelmed until we reached Garrity's gate and Mick handed her out of the car as if she were a departing duchess. I don't think she looked at me twice.

Later, frying eggs and canned beans in the same skillet, I tackled Mick about his concern for the literary development

76

of Dog Town and precincts. He had donned his old silver-framed spectacles and was peering owlishly into a ledger that had pretty red and blue lines carrying my uncle's flowing, copper-plate script.

"What's all this horse-shit about stimulating the burning minds of the Doolin kids, the Lynch brats and the Ryan faction?"

Mick regarded me benevolently over his eye-glasses. "The word is 'burgeoning.' Danny, you have yet to comprehend the deviousness of Irish politics. The fact is I've been a member of the School Board for years; this is not due to my essential popularity so much as to a canard extant in Brulé that I am educated. But my ambitions, at one time, soared to greater heights – I pined to be reeve of the township – an aspiration cruelly thwarted by Messrs Garrity & Co.

"You may not know Garrity. There are many in the world; Brulé is overstocked with them. He can neither read nor write; he can count. He guards the mill rate as the dog in Grimm's Fairy Tales guarded the treasure – the one with eyes as large as mill ponds. The new books in question strike deep into the treasury that Garrity thought safe from moths that devour and rust that corrupts."

"And gives the teacher a case of the google-eyes. . . ."

Mick tried his most disarming smile – the one showing his gold caps to the best advantage.

"I thought Miss Warren had striking eyes – not at all 'googly.' Don't you think our cuisine has fallen into a rut? Even catsup fails to disguise the eggs and beans."

I poked the handle of a table knife into the catsup bottle to dislodge the carcass of a fly that had crawled in and got himself drowned.

"Well, Rilance's ain't the A & P."

"Now that we have a limousine we could shop in Riverdale; perhaps even venture all the way to Lindsay and dine in splendour at the Broadway Café under the auspices of that noted chef and gourmet – Harry Lee Wong. We might even prevail on Miss Warren to accompany us; you could drive and. . . ."

"No!" I said violently.

"We could tackle one of these talking pictures," he went

on as if he hadn't heard me. He scraped the ruins of an egg into a tin pie-plate and set it before Fenris who destroyed it with a single gulp.

I got up and went outside and got some oats to feed the three horses. I left Mick to wash the dishes by himself.

SEVEN

May was gone and June had turned the corner. I looked forward to the fence-riding every morning. The pastures and woodlands were a solid sea of various shades of green, and the cattle were up to their hocks in grass through which the wind curried and waved until, from horseback, one had the impression the whole world was moving. The blossoms on the apple, chokecherry and saskatoon trees had dropped off, but the black haws stood smothered in white. The peepers around the ponds had quietened down, though already an occasional bull-frog was tuning up with the booming twang of a rubber band being plucked. Mud hens pumped belligerently as I rode by their hideaways in the tushy bogs.

On a morning after a night of rain when the big cumulus

clouds sailed high overhead like tufts of cotton batting, I was riding along the 10th line near the school house. Across from the school on Mick's ranch a scattering of quivering aspen clotted together to form several spinneys. I spotted Miss Warren and her gang of young thugs gathering flowers beneath the trees. I kneed Gertie into a lope and drew up with a pull on the reins that put her front legs in the air in the best Tom Mix style. The teacher had her arms full of wild flowers that set off the strawberries and cream of her complexion.

"I was just thinking of you," she cried. "I have that list of books prepared for your uncle. Can I give it to you, or perhaps your uncle could come and get it."

"I'll take it," I said quickly. Her eyes were delicate ovals fringed with dark lashes.

"Pickin' flowers, Miss Warren?"

"Oh yes, aren't they delightful – I've never seen violets growing so large. But you may call me Elaine. 'Miss Warren' makes you sound like one of my pupils."

"Well, I don't want to sound like one of them. That's a nice name – Elaine – sounds like buttercups and things. . . ."

"Why Danny! you Irish certainly have a strongly developed vein of poetry, don't you?"

I said I didn't know about that – I hadn't read much poetry.

"How far did you go in school?"

"Grade 8. Didn't get all the way through, though."

"The 8th Grade? Oh, I see; that's the equivalent of Senior Fourth here. Well, you must have taken some poetry."

I told her we had studied *Lady of the Lake* and a little bit of Tennyson and something about Longfellow.

" 'Tell me not in mournful numbers . . .' " Elaine recited. "Have you read Keats?"

"Nope," I fiddled with a bridle buckle.

"Goethe?"

"That's my horse's name."

She laughed merrily – a laugh like showers of silver dollars.

"Danny, why don't we get together sometime and discuss poetry and – and – well, all sorts of things: literature and art and the classics. . . ."

I rubbed my nose in embarrassment. I wanted to learn all about those things; most especially I wanted to get together with her and talk about anything, but I was mortally scared she would find out just how ignorant I really was and laugh at me. I wished I had Uncle Mick's easy grace and gift of gab; I wished I had his strong white teeth and wavy-rumpled silver hair. Much as I admired these attributes of my uncle I hated him for having them – for having such a way with women and school teachers so as to make them smile and dimple and set their eyes dancing.

The next Saturday forenoon saw me riding back to the school house where I had agreed to meet Miss Warren – Elaine – and start getting a first-hand acquaintance with poets, poetry and culture in general.

She ran down the school steps to meet me, wearing short blue shorts and a trim little white shirt open at the throat to show the rim of her white brassiere. Her legs were long, slender and had a good roll to the thighs. I couldn't remember having seen a girl, at least a girl as old as Elaine, in shorts before. I took a good long look so that she glanced down at her bare legs, ruefully self-conscious.

"It is *so* warm today . . . I suppose I'll shock the entire community with my display of 'nudity.' "

I wondered how anyone would set about shocking Slab Town and environs. I helped her over the fence, scenting, as I did so, that crushed wild thyme fragrance of her. Her hand, resting on my shoulder, burned through my denim shirt.

"Shall we walk? I can preach at you while we're walking. There's a truly beautiful pond just beyond those pine trees; it's a miniature lake, really, and it just cries to be explored."

The only crying I'd heard from the direction of that pond was made by a screech owl, but it was pretty place and I reckoned Elaine could only make it prettier by just being there.

"Did you give your uncle my list? He's a terribly fascinating man – just about the lone interesting male I've met around here. Oh – barring you, of course. Mr. Mulcahy seems to be very much of an unknown quantity in Brulé. I do think people are afraid of him. I know Mr. Garrity is – and dislikes him, probably for that reason," she pulled down the corners of her mouth in mimicry of Semper Garrity. " 'He be wun of duh mad Mulcahys, that bugger – Mick.' "

I would cheerfully have talked about any subject other than my uncle. "What book is that?" indicating the one she was carrying.

"*Greater English Poets.* It's a fairly standard text in the high schools. I feel you're quite a bit beyond Eugene Field and Pauline Johnson."

I nodded in agreement although I'd never heard of either person. That made things even – if I was beyond them they were equally beyond me.

The sun, high overhead, beat down strongly so that I was glad when we had threaded our way around the aspen spinneys and reached the cool, singing shade of a stand of white pine that grew right down to the edge of the pond. The pond was actually a small lake, being nearly the size of a one-acre plot. As we approached, a pair of mergansers flew up with a fine splash and whir of wings so that the mare threw up her head and danced around on the end of the reins by which I was leading her. I tethered Gertie to a pine bole and got some oats out of the saddle-bags to keep her contented and out of my hair.

Elaine had kicked off her sandals and was squidging her bare toes in the pond.

"Danny! come and see these lovely blue flowers. What are they? Aren't they wonderful?"

"Pickerel weed," I said with careless authority, having asked Uncle Mick the same question scarcely two days before.

"Oh dear, what a prosaic name for a flower. Why do unimaginative people name things the way they do?"

"Probably for the same reason they call us 'The Mad Mulcahys.' "

She shot me a swift glance.

"I'm very inclined to agree with you," she said soberly.

I lay on my back on a carpet of rusty pine needles slightly warmed where the sunlight came through in dapples. Elaine sat, tailor-fashion, holding her book in her lap, reading from Keats and Coleridge and Robert Browning. Under the lull of her voice, rising and falling in cadence, I felt drowsy. I sat up and rolled a smoke to keep awake.

I liked Keats the best, especially the part in *The Eve of St. Agnes* where Madeline –

> Unclasps her warmed jewels one by one;
> Loosens her fragrant bodice; by degrees
> Her rich attire creeps rustling to her knees;
> Half-hidden, like a mermaid in sea-weed,
> Pensive awhile she dreams awake, and sees,
> In fancy, fair St. Agnes in her bed,
> But dares not look behind or all the charm is fled.

I pictured Elaine removing her warmed jewels and letting her attire rustle to her knees. I peeped cautiously down the front of her shirt where the swell of her breasts pushed against the brassiere. I reached a straying hand and touched her knee; she caught my brown paw in her own white fingers and held it. She didn't flinch or shy away or shriek protests – just held my hand gently to halt the exploration.

About two in the afternoon, I walked with her back to the 10th road. After she was over the fence she turned and said, "Danny – I've had a wonderful day. And if you wish, there can be more – many more. I've a whole month before school is out for the summer and I have to go away."

My world clouded over. I'd clean forgot about the summer hiatus and I hadn't thought about Elaine ever going away. She saw the shadows shuttle across my eyes.

"But only for two months. I'm sure your uncle will use his influence to have my contract renewed. And I have to go to college this summer – I'm writing for my Master's, you know."

I didn't know. I didn't know what a Master's was. Right then I didn't give a good god damn, either. All I knew was that after thirty days Elaine would be gone and that riding fence along the 10th line would have no thrill for me. I wouldn't be able to strain my eyes for a look at a slender girl out pitching soft-ball for the kids, or a bright face with chestnutty hair at the window watching me ride by.

I swung into the saddle and looked after the teacher until

she was nothing but a blue and white dot along the gravel road. That night, lying sleepless on top of my bedding down by the creek, I heard the muted wail of trains somewhere along the north line – going west, going east, going anywhere. I never felt so lost and sad and lonesome in my life. I wished I was on a train, on a ship, on anything. I pressed my face into the sleeping bag and cried for the first time since my parents died.

The next week my uncle disappeared.

When he had been gone two days and nights without word, I commenced to worry. Wherever Mick had gone, he had taken the Plymouth and his banjo with him. On the third day I saddled Gertie and rode over to Horncastle to make inquiries. Rilance's was closed, it being their habit to shut the shop all day on Wednesdays, but I heard Charlie George clanging away at something over in his shop, so I reined up there.

Charlie was crouched over an anvil hammering out steel wedges for splitting cordwood; the shop was filled with the acrid stink of burning coke, singed horse hair and thirty years of non-ventilation. Charlie didn't look up when I approached and he didn't stop whacking at his wedges when I shouted that I was looking for my uncle and had he seen him. He just shook his head and with a pair of long-handled tongs dipped a hot wedge in a tub of greasy water. I could see I wasn't going to get much conversation and even less information out of Charlie. I went out and turned Gertie in the direction of home.

As I was passing the blacksmith's house, a voice called out. "Hi – hi! Hi you, there, young man! You on the horse!"

Being the only young man within the city limits and certainly the only young man on a horse, I deduced the summons was for me. I stopped and saw Mrs. George scuttling down the cracked concrete walk that led to their little iron gate.

She was a woman of about sixty, with a thin tangle of long hairs dangling from her chin. These, with her sly-looking, lead-coloured eyes, reminded me strongly of a mean-natured goat.

The Georges were a childless couple, although which of the

duo was barren I can't say. Maybe both. Whether this was a good thing for the kids they never had, I am likewise unsure. Mrs. George was a dabbler in every pool of fundamentalist doctrine she could find. She flew from Holy Roller to Duck River Baptist with side excursions into blue Methodism and Advents for Christ. By her tally a tidal wave of sin, starting somewhere around Dog Town, was sweeping across the township and threatening to engulf Horncastle. To stave off the flood Mrs. George had erected a dike of piety made of sandbags stuffed with prayer and Bible reading. For one who never left her threshold save to trot to Rilance's the woman was privy to every bedroom secret in five townships. She had an eye designed strictly for keyholes.

She came up with a haste that made her beard wobble.

"If you're looking for that uncle of yours," she panted, "you ain't likely to find him here."

I pointed out that I didn't expect to.

"Wait–" and her eyes twinkled with delicious malice. "Maybe you ought to look for him over in Slab Town."

I said that Slab Town was a mighty big place – almost twenty or thirty houses – and did she figure I should tap-tap on each and every door and say, "Please sir, have you seen Mr. Mulcahy?"

"Just go to Burke's. Some calls him 'Red John.' He's the big bootlegger over there you know. P'lice is after him all the time. Keeps evil wimmen around, too."

I touched my hat, thanked her, said any place that sold booze and kept bad women would be the last spot I would likely find a Christian gentleman such as my uncle, and trotted away.

It was about high onto noon when I dropped anchor outside of Red John Burke's. I didn't need to inquire which deadfall belonged to the bootlegger; I could hear Mick's banjo as soon as I cantered into the town limits.

Red John was the possessor of the sole two-storied house in town. It was a large, rooky-looking frame affair that had been built in better days and survived to shelter Burke and his entourage. Perhaps some mill-owner or lumber king with more money than prescience had erected the house. If you looked close you could see that the narrow clapboards had once been painted white, although now the white had weathered into a venomous grey-green.

I tethered the mare and clumped up the rickety steps onto an open verandah sporting cracked and broken gingerbread around the fringes. I tested my knuckles on the screen door and a frightful-looking cat jumped in through a hole in the bottom of the door which seemed to have been put there just for that purpose. There was a considerable hurrah going on inside, although I couldn't hear the banjo, so I hammered louder.

A heavy-set, chesty fellow of about fifty swaggered to the door and gave me a hard eye through the remnants of screening. He wore a stained singlet through which protruded tufts of iron red hair. He was as bald as a cantaloupe except for a monkish fringe of thatch the same colour as that on his chest.

"What th'fuck you want? Do I know you? Have I seen you before?"

"I don't want anything from you. Tell Mick Mulcahy I want to talk to him."

"He ain't here, me bucko. Now just turn around and toddle back to wherever it is you came from before I come out and spank you." He hooked his thumbs in the waist of his pants and pulled an ugly face for my benefit.

I stepped back to give myself punching room. "I saw his car around at the back and I heard his banjo. Come on out and start spanking."

Red John, at least I figured him to so be, let out a bawl and bulled through the door. I didn't give him time to bear-hug me with those meaty arms that were covered with rusty fur; I drop-kicked him right where his belly sagged over his greasy trousers, and when he bent over with a whoosh of air as if he was looking for something he'd dropped, I brought my knee up with a smart crack that was aimed at breaking his nose but went too wide and bounced off the knot of his head. He sat down heavily, fighting to regain his wind; he looked up at me dully as if wondering from what cloud the cyclone had fallen.

"*Wheeee-yewwwww!* it takes a Mulcahy to beat the bad manners out of you, John. . . ."

Mick was standing in the door, banjo in one hand, grinning

at the wreck of Red John. I had never seen him so drunk. His hair was rumpled and sweat rolled from his hair-line down his face. He swayed and steadied himself against the door frame.

"Allow me to introduce the last, and perhaps the maddest, of the Mulcahys: I give you Daniel Xavier Cornelius Mulcahy."

The bootlegger got to his feet. "Whyncha say who you were?. . . Comin' to a man's house and knockin' him around."

Mick grabbed my arm with a hand like a vise and pulled me inside.

"And who gave you licence to play nurse-maid to me?" His grip tightened until my arm began to numb.

Mick's eyes were flat and hard-looking; there was no laughter in them. I felt scared, but mad, too.

"Let go or you'll get what your bootlegger buddy got." I jerked at his hold, kicking at his kneecap at the same time.

His free hand fell like a clap of thunder on the side of my face. The pain, for an instant, almost made me throw up. I sagged at the knees and threw up an arm to ward off another slap, but Mick released me and shoved me staggering over against a wall. Burke had re-entered the house and he loosed a hyena-like snicker. Mick turned on him.

"Why, John. . . . Good to see you up and about. Tell us the point of the joke, John, so we can all giggle. Maybe. . . ."

"Now, god dammit, Mick, go easy. I didn't mean nothin'. Me gut's sore, Mick. I've had me enough rowin' for one day.

"Play us another tune, Mick, and we'll have a drink. Does the young fellow take a drink. I'll set up the drinks this time."

Mick was his old, suave self again. He ran a thick hand through his hair. A stout woman about the age of Burke was standing in a doorway that led to the kitchen; Mick leered at her.

"Danny – Mrs. Madeline Burke. You've met her good husband, I believe."

Mrs. Burke was almost as pretty as her husband. She provided me with a gap-toothed smile I'd just as soon she'd kept. She wiped red hands on the hem of her dress.

"Maddy – get us some beer, here." The lord of the mansion was himself again although there was a raw, red streak where my knee had connected with the side of his pate.

While we were drinking beer and getting acquainted, a couple of men knocked at the screen and were admitted to the group. One was a short man of forty; the other was younger, taller and just as unimpressing. I learned that the short one was Garnet Gifford; the other was a Pat Marren.

Later, two women, one of whom seemed to be the wife of Pat Marren, came in. The house was beginning to fill with customers.

The beer was bitter and flat to the taste; I nursed my bottle as long as I could so that I wouldn't be pressed to drink more. The air inside that house was dismal with tobacco smoke, stale beer and cheap toilet water. Everyone was drinking too much too fast and laughing too loudly as if they were bound and bent on having a good time and all hell wasn't going to prevent them from doing it. I couldn't understand why my uncle would want to waste time in such a stifling hole among a bunch of run-down, worked-over citizens. He sat in the middle of everything like the Great God Pan with that saturnine smile on his face, while the women shrieked at his sallies whether they understood them or not and the men shook their heads and foolishly grinned their admiration. I commenced to realize that here in Slab Town, and maybe around all of Brulé, Uncle Mick was a kind of King Frog in a puddle big enough for him to operate in and small enough to rule out any possible competitors. Physically and mentally, the man was head and shoulders over this crowd or anyone else I had met so far around Brulé; Mick knew it and he reveled in it; doted on it. I could admire him for his superiority without respecting him in that way, the same as I could admire his way of tracking down Toot Finnerty without respecting the reasons he had for doing it.

Mick was warming up the banjo, trailing out a few catchy chords, while the others nodded their heads or thumped their hands in rhythm. He struck a note and showed his gold caps:

> Old Missus Hanrahan
> Out pickin' peas –
> Hair from her pussy-cat
> Hung to her knees.

The Marren woman and the other female, whose name may have been Myrtle or Mabel or something, squealed and slapped their thighs, letting their knees fly up to show a peek at the Promised Land should anyone care to look. But to demonstrate how easy it is to misjudge strangers, Pat Marren, who I had carelessly looked over and set down as two-tenths of a point above an imbecile, got up and stood behind Mick's chair and joined him in a singing duet. Pat had just about the sweetest tenor I'd ever heard for country singing until, in after years, Roy Acuff came along. That kind of high, wild voice chimed perfectly with Mick's easy baritone, with Mick sticking to the main air and Pat going high on the tail-endings and the chorus. They sang a sad, pretty mountain song about some Blue Ridge feud:

> Down by the river
> The willow grows tall;
> Late in the evening –
> Hear the whip-poor-wills call.
>
> High on the mountain –
> Outlined on the hill
> Sits a wild horseman;
> He'll murder and kill. . . .

I forget how it all goes now, but that's the beginnings. I'd never heard better singing than that on the radio and it must have caught the feelings of the listeners, because their faces grew pensive and one of the women wiped her eyes a few times.

Red John, drinking enough to fancy himself Irish and a rough customer, lumbered through a kind of jig which was more startling than graceful. He called for an Irish song, so Mick obliged:

> I was born one day in a place called Green Erin
> Where the whiskey and shillings are plenty, they say;
> Where the boys all are charmers – the girls all are darlins'
> And the Seventeenth of March, sure you all know the day.
> All my days and my nights I spent merry and frisky
> 'Til I fell in love with one Biddy Malone;
> Her father kept a still-house and made poteen whiskey
> And I did the same in sweet Illaighnahone.

Along onto supper time I dug out without anyone seeming to notice I was leaving and rode home. Gertie was hungry, having gnawed a clean circle around the place I'd had her tied. I felt ashamed at having her go hungry and unwatered while I was sitting drinking beer in Red John's catch-all. As soon as I got home I gave the mare a double feed of oats and bran and rubbed her down and curried her. Then I set to and scrubbed out the lived-in part of the house with a fury. I didn't much care if Mick stayed in Slab Town forever. Besides, I'd a notion I wanted the place looking clean and tidy in case we had distinguished visitors sometime – like maybe Elaine Warren. But that didn't happen. Not for awhile.

EIGHT

The school teacher and I got together twice more for study sessions, as she called them, before the two-month summer holiday came along at the end of June. I had invited her over to share a bachelor dinner with Mick and me, but she declined without appearing too brusque about it. On looking back, I can see she would hardly think it a good idea to gallivant off and spend time with a couple of strange males, especially when those males were the mad Mulcahys. Mrs. Charlie George would have had a field day with that one. Yet, I did feel a little hurt that Elaine seemed to have other things to do and that the only place we could meet and talk was out in the back pastures.

When her school closed, I drove Elaine all the way to Beaverton to catch her train. It was the first time I had ever driven so far and I was torn between elation at a round-trip drive and sorrow because Elaine was leaving for two months. Up to that time she was the nicest thing that had come into my life; she had given me a glimpse into a life I had known only through storybooks. She banished "ain'ts" from my growing vocabulary; I learned to make verbs agree with their subjects. I also discovered the existence of more renowned poets than Edgar Guest and Walt Mason.

Uncle Mick was in the front yard when I got back; his slouch hat was pulled low over his eyes, which was a habit of his when he was thinking. If he realized I was feeling down in the mouth he didn't let on; besides, it was his suggestion I take Elaine to Beaverton.

"Do you believe, Danny, that an object without life may have evil properties we cannot understand?"

I thought he was hurrahing me, but there was no tell-tale glint in his eyes.

"That house, now . . . I'm beginning to think I dislike it. I've lived in it for some years; in fact I wasn't much more than a baby when we came here from the old country. We lived in a log house at first – you've seen the cellar hole out back of where the clothesline runs. The old man went into debt to put up this monstrosity for the sake of some woman he was sweet on at the time. He had several women that came and went. My sister – your great-aunt – Rosie kept house and looked after John and me.

"The year I was thirteen and Rosie was eighteen, she met one of the co-owners of the Coughlin & Rice Lumber Company: Alphonse Rice. They were married that fall right here at Riverdale. The old man was annoyed because he lost his free housekeeper, nursemaid and girl-of-all-chores.

"Father, despite his foolishness with women, was astute enough to realize land like this would never respond to tillage. He had been a small time grazier in Ireland and he knew cattle as he knew the back of his hand. He began to make money just about as fast as he could spend it. He had his mind set on sending John and me to college. John, however, had a wild streak; he got a girl – your grandmother – in the family way and they married. She was a Farrel – Veronica Farrel.

"When John was killed, Veronica came here with the two boys. I was away much of the time, then, attending university – took a General Arts degree which may or may not surprise you (the old man wanted me to be a lawyer). Rosie was living in Philadelphia, her husband being an American. She has been dead now for seven or eight years.

"Veronica and father were at loggerheads continuously; finally she took Patsy and left, leaving Con with the old man. It didn't have a beneficent effect on Con.

"The rest you are familiar with. I knocked about for many years until father died leaving this place to Rosie and me jointly. I mortgaged my share and bought Rosie out. After a time I bought that five hundred acres fronting on the river."

He flipped his cigarette stub into a patch of clover; there was a sad, haunted look to his eyes I hadn't noticed there before. I wondered if being King Frog in the Brulé puddle was as satisfying as I had figured it to be.

The next day I set out for the Longford Rocks for a month's work at cutting beaver hay. . . .

While most cattle raisers in that part of the county grew their own hay, it entailed a considerable body of work: fields had to be cultivated and sowed to clover such as alsike or red and white clover. The land had to be fertilized and the crops rotated. Growing your own feed that way also meant keeping a fair assortment of implements. Mick got his winter's supply of hay from an outfit with long holdings and short finances back in Longford Township at the extreme northern tip of the county. The Rocks of Longford lay wholly within the Canadian Shield and, depending on how you looked at it, it was a country of god-forsaken wasteland or the prettiest place on earth. Great rounded granite hummocks rolled for miles from horizon to horizon – like an undulating red sea with here and there clumps of scrub oak or a few dots of poplar. Where the red granite wasn't as bare as a bird's ass, a thick whiskering of blueberry bushes covered the terrain. In between the hummocks, in swales which dried up by late spring, grew a kind of grass that was sharp and juicy; this was called beaver hay on account of those animals damming the streams that occasionally connected the swale holes, and the swales were called beaver meadows. There were no beaver left, they having been long trapped out, and some of the meadows would be maybe only the size of a one-acre plat; others would cover as much as ten or twelve acres. Rough and coarse, and often mixed with wild carrot, yarrow and brown-eyed susan, beaver hay made fairly good feed when cut at the right time, dried and stacked. It may not have been as good as the best of alfalfa, but such hay was cheap, required no special tillage and it had plenty of natural nutrients on which wintering beeves thrived.

My uncle, for some years, had dickered with a rock-squatter named Cully Dallan, buying beaver hay for a dollar a ton. Mick sent his own crew in to do the cutting, raking and hauling. The Longford Rocks was pretty well all Crown land, although the Crown in the shape of the Province of Ontario had about as much interest and concern for that neck of the woods as they had for the rings around Saturn.

Haying was a business I was experienced at, having worked at it in the summertime since I was big enough to handle a three-tined fork. We were up at dawn, loading the hay-rack onto a wagon bed and loading that with the mower, sacks of feed oats for the horses, a patched tent for sleeping out, and odds and ends of accessories I'd need such as extra cutter guards and a spare mower knife. We packed on a grindstone – a huge white emery wheel set in a frame that was powered by someone sitting on the frame and operating a treadle. Food supplies would be bought later on at Horncastle. We hooked the hay rake behind the rack wagon and hitched the work team – Dolly and Fly – to the wagon. George Heeney walked over from his shack after breakfast; Mick had hired him to help me – a crew I could have done without except that Mick said the old goat needed the money and that he wasn't too bad a hand when he was sober and that it was my responsibility to see he stayed sober, at least during the day. My uncle had arranged to have some of the Dallan boys crew in with George and me and to provide an extra team when needed. I tied Gertie by the halter shank to the seat of the rake and headed for Longford and the beaver meadows.

The Dallan layout was to the north of Brulé and somewhat in from the east-west road that led to Dog Town and suburbs.

The fast-running Black River, of which the Culm was a tributary, snaked through the granite south of the Dallan place, its course traced out by the alder and scrub pine lining its route. Heeney knew the set-up, having worked for Mick before; he showed me where to pitch the camp and set up our gear. We took our time at it – we'd be there for a month.

I left George to dine in splendour out of a can of beans accompanied by chunks of baker's bread worried off a loaf with his old clasp knife he used for trimming his toe-nails and picking his teeth, and rode Gertie across a rough log bridge spanning the Black until I fetched up at Dallan's. It wasn't much when I got there and a man wouldn't pay good money to go and see it if he didn't have to. An old log house of two stories squatted fairly on the brow of a rock knob as bald as Heeney's head. There were some tattered outbuildings, also of log, some of them still sporting trough roofs dating from pioneer times when hollow logs were clasped one inside the other to keep out half the rain at least.

As I rode into the manure-spattered yard I was surrounded by a mixed reception committee of tow-headed kids and blue-tick hounds, all of them jumping and leaping and baying so I couldn't make out one from another. Cully Dallan strode out of his front door, spitting a long cud of tobacco at the rear end of the hound nearest to him. Dallan was a beanpole of a man, maybe fifty or more, with a shock of grey-roan hair that looked as if someone had got at it with a dull bread-knife. He wore a pair of dirty bib overalls and a set of long johns gone yellow with age. His feet were bare.

"Good-day to you. How are yuh, anyhow. Been lookin' for you to come along. Les – get away from that gawd damn horse before it kicks the balls off you. . . . Yuh ate yet? Get down, get down – the old woman's got the grub on the table. . . . Mary – for the luv of dyin' jesus get out of the man's road and let him light. Shut up! Christ on a hand-car! – you can't hear yourself think around here for dogs and kids!"

I gave the mare in charge of a corporal's guard of youngsters who led her off toward one of the log barns with the admonition from their father to grain her and give her a good dab of hay or he'd boot their collective arses so hard and high they'd be wearing them for necklaces for the next six months. The kids paid about as much attention to these black threats as they did to the whooping of the hounds who, having smelled and sniffed and yowled themselves tired, collapsed in the shade of a box elder, managing to look stone dead but ready to come alive just as soon as Providence sent some other brand of excitement their way.

Dallan hauled me into a low-ceilinged kitchen and introduced me to his wife – a red-faced, tired-looking woman with the appearance of having borne too many children and of standing too long over a smoky kitchen range while her husband spattered tobacco juice on the stove lids. I was set at the end of the table that had a worn, but clean, red checked oil cloth. The table was long enough to entertain a crew of threshers; considering the number of Dallans that ate from it, the table wasn't any too commodious at that. While the old lady was getting the food off the stove and into platters, I got introduced around to the fry which, insofar as I can recollect, numbered nine, ranging from Toomey, the eldest at twenty-one, down to a rag-headed crawler whose name and title escapes me. In order of descending years there were Toomey, Blake, Fin, Holly, Drake, Mary, Les, Cale and the moppet whose name and sex were not easily determined. Maybe they hadn't got around to naming it at all at that time.

There was no mistaking the sex of the oldest girl – Holly. She was helping her mother set out the meal, casting appraising glances at me out of the edges of her eyes when she thought I wasn't looking and turning her head sharply away whenever I looked in her direction and caught her at it. Holly was about sixteen with the nicest pair of tanned legs showing below the hem of a too-short dress that may have fitted her two years ago. She had a combing of wild, resin-coloured hair that bounced and swirled around her shoulders as she moved between the stove and the table. I was disappointed after the round dozen of us took up our place mats and Holly elected to sit three kids away from me and I had to make do with rubbing elbows against the lanky Toomey and Drake, whose mouth was always open as though he was about to laugh or yodel or both.

If the food wasn't precisely of the Hotel Metropole variety, it was well-cooked and substantial: there was side-pork fried crisp and curling with the rind showing tiny bubbles; there were hash-browned potatoes, fried turnips, leaf lettuce swimming in milk and seasoned with vinegar. There was home-baked bread, and butter as yellow as daisies and tasting pleasantly rank of yarrow and crowfoot. For dessert we had chunks of apple pie done up in cinnamon syrup and smothered with cream. I was surprised to see how well-stocked a table that family provided considering the low-caste look to the general surroundings. I was to discover that they kept hogs, ran a few sheep, a handful of milk cows, and enough laying hens to provide eggs to go with their home-smoked bacon in the mornings. The Dallans sold hay, worked in the sawmills and at odd-jobbing. If they weren't landed gentry, they were a long way ahead of the Slab Town and Dog Town genre; the manners of the Dallans were rough but, somehow, musical.

While we were eating, Cully gave me some top advice on how to handle the haying project.

"You kin have Toomey and Blake, there; they're good hands and your uncle would be the first to tell you. If I was you I'd start in close to where you got your camp. The best thing is for you to do a day's mowing before you start to rake. There's a chain of swale holes close to your camp and they'll give you cuttin' enough for a day. There's some as rakes right after the mower, but was I you I'd let her lay fer a day or so and let the sun get at her and cure her good before you rake her. You won't need the boys 'til come day after tomorrow – you got old Bindle-nuts there with you to help if you need a hand."

He turned around and squinted up at the sky through a window curtained with undyed flour sacks on which could be seen ROBIN HOOD FLOUR and a picture of a guy in a green suit fixing to let fly with an arrow and a bow.

"She's gonna be fair for a few days, though I seen me a dog around the moon last night and she's been pretty warm. . . . We'll get a whoor of a big thunder storm less'n a week be out. What's old Mick doin' with himself? – watchin' the cattle beasts, I s'pose. Say, do you want a beer before you start back? I'd send some along with you but that old piss-cutter of a Heeney would drink'm all before you cut the froth on the first bottle."

97

I hitched the work team to the mower, oiled the running parts with a spout-can and headed the clanking machine for the nearest beaver meadow. I eased the rig in, dropped the cutter bar and set the pitman in motion. I cut counter to the clock on the first two complete rounds around the perimeter of the swale. When I had cut out a couple of bar widths, I reversed direction so that the team and the mower would travel over cut-over ground and not trample down the spear-pointed grass. The sun shone hot and fairly, bringing the sweat out on the horses, drying in salt patches beneath the harness. There was a good smell in the air of juicy grass and pungent yarrow and Queen Anne's lace. The team pulled with a will, throwing their heads up and down to ward away the bottle flies shimmering about their noses. Their thick lips dripped steadily of green ooze around the bits.

Hawks sailed overhead, crying shrilly, breasting whatever updrafts they could find on strong, brown wings. A settlement of crows made a fuss over in the pines skirting the river; I figured them to be on some murder raid or perhaps they'd found a sleepy owl to torment. An occasional meadowlark whistled at me from a grassy place high on the surrounding rocks, and warblers darted in and out of the huckleberry bushes. Once, a red fox scouting along with his nose to some scent trail paused and looked me over, one paw raised delicately in the air. Then he was gone in a tawny flash, bounding as effortlessly as blown thistle-down over the rim of the granite, his plume waving jauntily to the last.

By six o'clock the horses were tired and made no objections when I stopped the rig in the middle of cutting out the second swale and unhitched them. George had the tent up, the sleeping bags laid out and supper going on a portable kerosene stove. His culinary imagination didn't run much past hashing up fried eggs and beans swallowed down with coffee made with river water, he being a mite too lazy to drag all the way to Dallan's for well water. Still, I've eaten worse and I was hungry. We ate supper and listened to the purr of the river and the grumping of a bittern downstream where a mess of cattails grew in a water hole formed in a quiet jog where the river rose in flood to subside by summer. Heeney had set up the tent under a spanning of aspen. After we had eaten, George stretched out on his bedding with a book; I remembered, with annoyance, I had forgotten to bring anything at all in the line of reading material. I peeked over at the torn cover of George's book; it was *Frank James on the Trail of Bob Ford.* I left him with his bank robbers and back shooters and strolled down the river bank for a piece. The sun had set and the night air was filled with the humming of a million flying insects, a fair percentage of them determined to light on me and take home a chunk to feed the kids. A few late robins ran across the rocks, sounding lonely and sad at nightfall. In the distance a northbound train called long and softly from the direction of Bracebridge. That sounded lonesome too. I wondered about Elaine and who she'd be seeing and maybe going out with. I wished the summer was over and she was back at the 10th Concession school and walking with me about the ranch and telling me all about painters and great writers like Joyce and Proust. I felt sad and alone and away from everything. Then I thought of Holly Dallan's warm brown knees and the hint of brown, marbled thighs. A wolf howled from a ridge a long way off; he was answered by one of his friends nearer the river. I turned and walked back to the camp. I fell asleep to the tune of the gurgling river and the snores of old Heeney. I could have parted company with the latter without regret.

A blue heron awakened me in the morning. The sun was just beginning to flare above the horizon, shining through the worn canvas of the tent. The heron was flying up-river in the direction of the sun; he squawked as he flapped over the camp, and there are worse ways of being rousted out of bed in the morning.

A million birds sang up and down the river. The horses, tied to trees, stamped heavily and pawed the blueberry bushes at their feet, indicating they were hungry. I led them to the river where they drank deeply, tossing their heads and letting the cool water slosh out of their mouths. When they were fed, I kicked the side of the tent where George was still bugling through his hairy nose, unaware of birds, horses or the singing river running for the glory of the day.

"Daylight in the swamp – drop your cock and grab your sock!"

While the old man was muttering and coughing his way into his dirty clothing, I found a point of rock jutting out into the river. I sat there, leaning back on my elbows in the blueberry bushes on which some fruit was beginning to ripen. The morning breeze, gentle and not yet heated up by the action of the sun glaring almost straight down on naked rocks, stirred through the leaves of the scrub oak. The breeze felt cool on my face. Downstream, a muskrat dropped into the Black with a splash; he angled across the river, making hard going of it against the current. It felt wonderful just to be alive on such a day. I admired my reflection in the river showing a tanned, hard torso and good muscles running along my arms and shoulders.

On the morning of our third day in the hay camp, the Dallan boys, Toomey and Blake, drove in with an extra team. We laid out the operation so that Toomey handled the hay rake while Blake and George took the raked coils of beaver grass and stacked them into four-foot high mounds, called "cocks" in that part of the country. After the hay-cocks had cured in the sun and wind for a few days they were loaded on the wagon rack and stacked on Dallan land across the river near the Dog Town road. In the winter, when there was little to do around the ranch except to poke oak knots into the box stove, the hay was trailed home on the rack which was fitted to bob-sleighs and either stored in the big mows inside the barn or fed directly to the wintering cattle in the feed yard next to the barn.

When the sun was just about straight up and down, we laid off for the noon meal. As we were graining the horses, Toomey, an even lankier but much better-looking version of his father, said his maw expected me up for dinner.

"I can't rightly do that. I had one meal there already. We've plenty of eats even if George does mangle them somewhat."

"Why, Toomey'n me figured we'd eat with ole George there," Blake put in, and I noticed how the Dallans had sky-blue eyes that always seemed to be laughing.

That seemed like a fair enough trade for me, although I didn't consider the Dallan lads came out even in the shuffle. Anyway, I left them digging joyously into cold pork and beans, cold chunks of bologna and tinned apricots, while I trotted up the trail to have dinner with their family.

Cully and I sat around the red-clothed table drinking beer while we waited for the dinner to be served. I had stopped along the trail, having seen a clump of wild sweet-briar rose growing from a cleft in the granite where the rains had washed down some top soil and rock crumbs so that growing things like roses and columbines and little wild blue elfin-bells could get a toe-hold and prosper. With my stock-knife I whittled off a few select sprays of sweet-briar, and when I got to the Dallans' I held them out to the old woman. Her face rosied up and for the first time I saw her eyes smile the way those of her children did.

"Why now – that was real thoughtful of you. I just don't hardly recall when anybody ever brung me flowers before. And roses, too! I just dearly love the smell of roses, I do."

She buried her face in the pink blossoms and for a moment she looked like the pretty girl she once must have been a long time back.

The girl – Holly – set the table, putting the dishes and utensils down with a flourish; returning to the old-fashioned sideboard with a twist of her hips that set her gingham dress swirling about her legs. On her feet was a pair of boy's canvas sneakers – foot-gear badly designed to bring out the best features of the female leg. Holly's legs stood the test, even in sneakers. I fought to keep my eyes off the twinkling knees and my thoughts on what her father was spouting.

"How' ja like that beer? cold enough for yuh? Keep it down the well in a gunny-sack." The beer was icy cold. The bottles were covered with beads of cool condensation.

"How's that mower cuttin'? That's a good mower: Frost & Wood. I mind when Mick bought her; must be four – no – maybe five years ago. Frost & Wood turns out a good mower. You take Massey-Harris, now. . . . Holly! you got you a rip in the rear of that dress showin' half your back-side. Lord snappin' jesus! I don't mind the real young uns runnin' around half naked. . . . 'T'ain't decent for a girl that age to be showin' the cheeks of her ass – not in this part of the country. Some of these wild young skites see yuh like that out on the rocks, they'll pull yuh in behind the bushes and have it up yuh before you kin holler 'Sweet Virgin Mary.' "

Trying to get a peek at that interesting rip in the dress, I just about dislocated a neck bone. I thought about pulling Holly in behind a scrub oak thicket and feeling the squirm of those brown legs going around my back. I blushed and made out to be studying the label on the beer bottle real hard. Holly wasn't fooled any; she tilted her head defiantly and stuck her tongue out at me, but her eyes were wide and smiling and as blue as the noon sky.

Mrs. Dallan had gotten together a garden dinner of radish and crisp leaf lettuce and beefsteak tomatoes. To go with these there was potato salad and rounds of smoked ham and scalding tea fresh off the fire. After that we had hot biscuits with saskatoon-berry preserves. I hadn't tasted saskatoon preserves since I'd left Alberta. I had three helpings and wished I'd had the nerve to ask for more.

Holly was to go to the hay camp with me, bringing a stone jug of well water into which a handful of oatmeal had been thrown. The jug was wrapped in wet sacking to keep it cool.

"You might as well get on the horse," I said to the girl. "You can hang the jug from the saddle horn."

"And what are you going to do – climb up behind me?" Her eyes danced with mischief.

"I'll walk alongside and look at the scenery."

She pouted at me and made to scramble into the saddle from the wrong side. I showed her how to put her left foot in the stirrup, and I took her other foot in my two hands and heaved her smartly onto the mare. There was a flash of white underpants, startling and seductive against the berry-brown of her body. There was a queer tugging at my groin. I thought of Elaine and how she had looked in shorts that first day we walked out to the pond together. Elaine's legs were long and white and classically moulded, with a network of tiny blue veins on the bottom of her thighs showing when she sat with her legs pulled up and her chin resting on her knees. I compared them silently with Holly's legs, now bared halfway to her body as she sat astraddle Gertie. Holly's legs were brown and witchy

– the colour of a Rhode Island hen's eggs – and just as smooth. It made a pleasant journey back to the camp.

That evening, George and I sat by the river while the dusk dropped slowly like the dust from a moth's wings, creeping in over the rocks and gaining a thicket here and an outcropping there. The old man had rigged up a fishing pole and line; every so often he'd lift up the pole and examine the hook, shake his head and drop it back into the stream.

"Them Dallans are some outfit," he informed me. "They call them 'The Wild Dallans.'"

"Well, we're known as the 'Mad Mulcahys.'"

A kingfisher swooped across the water with a rattling cry. Heeney jerked his pole up sharply, landing the fish wriggling on the end of the line with a thump.

"Damn sucker," he complained, bending to squint at his catch in the fading light. He squeezed a ball of bologna onto the hook and tossed the line into the current.

"They say Trudy used to be quite the gal before she married Cully. Some say she was still good for a quick jump after, too. Could be all them tads running around the yard ain't their dad's get."

"With all that free tail roaming around these rocks it's a living wonder you weren't grinding a path to get at it."

"Hah! I got my share when it was going. Trudy was too young for me, though. She was a Jowett – Cackling Jack Jowett's daughter. They lived in Longford, too, but down the line a piece. Bunch o' rock runners same as the Dallans."

"Why was he called Cackling Jack?"

"Oh, I did hear why that was, but I forget. Say, ain't that oldest girl that was here a getsome piece! I'd love to get it into her and break it off."

I looked at him. He was a foul old man a lot closer to the grave than to the cradle, sitting there hooking river suckers that were too bony and wormy to be eaten, but that old blister would rather deprive a fish of life or a kingfisher or otter of a meal than sit quietly and watch the flow of the river and listen to the red-winged blackbirds crying *"Oke-a-leee!"* His dirty grey moustache hadn't been washed or wiped since he started growing it; his clothes were steeped in undisturbed grime. Yet he talked about getting his whang into a lively, comely young girl like Holly Dallan as if he was accustomed to knocking it off with a sixteen-year-old filly every day of the week. Perhaps in his inner mind Heeney knew very well he was pretending to a throne that for him didn't exist. Maybe a man never gets too old or too scruffy that he doesn't imagine some woman somewhere will lie down and open her legs for him. Whatever it was, I didn't like the way the old fool laid his tongue on the Dallans, and especially on Holly.

I lay awake for a long time that night, watching, through the screening against which the miller-moths bumped and fluttered and the mosquitoes droned in frustrated fury, the near-to-full moon climbing steadily into the inky-blue sky. I lay on my sleeping bag and had visions of Elaine and Holly running across my sight with their skirts flouncing high on their bare legs. The last thing I heard was a whippoorwill down in the pine thickets, calling, calling, far into the moon-filled night.

After the second week, the Dallan boys began drawing the hay out near the road line where they built great mounds of stacks looking like gigantic sugar-loafs. George could do one thing well and that was he knew how to build and trim a hay stack. I continued to mow, working the team about ten hours a day, moving from swale to swale that was dry enough to cut. Beaver grass is tough and can take the edge off a mower knife in a single day. In the evening, while George cussed and washed the dishes, I sat astride the grindstone frame and sharpened the knife blades one by one.

About noon one Saturday, when I was mowing in a swale about a mile north and east of camp, Holly came scampering over the rocks carrying a basket in one hand and the stoneware jug in the other. She was wearing a sparkling-clean white linen dress that made her skin glow an even deeper tan. I hauled up Fly and Dolly, wrapping the lines around a gear handle.

"They told me back at the camp you were cutting up this way, so here I am and I've found you," she cried breathlessly.

"I'm glad you're here and that you've found me." The perspi-

104

ration streamed down my shoulders and trickled through the beginning of a mat of black fuzz sprouting from my chest. I *was* glad and my lop-sided grin showed it.

While I unhitched the team and poured hulled oats out of a bag into a couple of beat-up granite dishes for them, Holly located a grassy stretch in the shade of a white oak that had somehow found a place to get its roots down and squeeze sufficient nourishment to grow into a respectable tree. I watered the horses at a mud ooze at one end of the swale and joined Holly under the oak. She had spread a little white cloth and set out flour biscuits sliced in half with a piece of cold, fried side-meat in between the halves. She had brought fresh radishes and green onions with salt to dip them in, and a jar of her mother's wine-red saskatoon preserves.

Holly kneeled on the grass, sitting back on her heels so that her dress was tugged well above her knees. She patted the grass beside her.

"Sit down and have some of these biscuits; I made them fresh this morning – just for you." She favoured me with her soft blue gaze.

"Maw says I've a great old crush on you – isn't that foolish of her? It's just that you seem different to the boys around here. They're such rowdies! The ones I went to school with at Longford School were just . . . well, they were just awful. I've been out of school going on two years now."

The water in the jug was cold and sweet with the oatmeal that had been added. I drank heavily, keeping my near eye on the round bloom of Holly's knees.

"You must be getting tired of eating what that terrible old Heeney man cooks for you."

"He isn't exactly a chef par excellence." I tried to make the "par excellence" sound the way Uncle Mick did, remembering he had used that selfsame term to describe my own cooking talents.

"Say, that sounds French," she said, around a mouthful of biscuit and pork. "Do you speak French?"

I modestly admitted to picking up a little of this and that on my world travels, without having due and utter regard for the facts.

105

"It must be exciting to travel around and see all the different places," Holly sighed. "I seldom get to Lindsay, even. I was to Toronto once – a long time ago when I was a little girl. We went into Eaton's. Have you ever been in Eaton's? Such a big store! I ran through all the aisles and up and down – just looking. . . ."

As we ate, a rumbling sounded from the west; it appeared to be far away and seemed hollow. I stood up, scanning the skyline; I couldn't see any cloud sign, but the sky at ground level was a dark, grape-coloured hue. Holly thought it was Toomey and Blake coming with the hay wagon. I shook my head.

"*Nuh uh*. The sky looks dark over there. Besides, they're having their dinner right now at the camp." As if to prove me right, the sky boomed again, longer this time, and not so hollow.

"If that storm hits, we'll be laid up for a few days, I suppose." I dug into the preserves.

Holly was sitting with her legs stretched out, supporting herself with her arms as she leaned back. The sun, dappling through the motionless leaves, played dancing games up and down the warmth of her legs. I commenced to experience a very embarrassing phenomenon in the lower region of my anatomy. I sprang to my feet and moved a few steps away.

"God damn it! do you have to sit like that?" I raged.

Her eyes widened and she opened her mouth as if to say something, but nothing came out. She just stared at me, her lips parted and her head shaking from side to side. I turned, flinging down beside her. I pulled her to me and crushed my mouth against hers; my hand was hard against the satin of her thigh; I pushed my hand further up, wishing she might resist me before I went too far, but she locked her arms around my neck and spread her legs wider.

The way they write about these things in the true romance magazines is a lot different, as far as I am concerned, to the actual state of affairs as they come about. In the story books the male and female make love in a kind of rosy glow with sun-bursts and blazing stars. Maybe I just never moved in the right circles to make the acquaintance of that brand of sex, because at first, with Holly, there was a lot of fumbling and some clumsy rolling around before we ever got down to the essentials. Suddenly she gripped her lower lip hard with her teeth and her thighs clung to me . . . I felt an obstruction, momentarily, then the realization came to me that Holly was a virgin and what was I ever going to do about the whole business now.

I was no caballero, gay or otherwise, at that time and I'm not yet, but I knew enough about the birds and bees and the way of how babies come to be born so that I stopped up short, albeit with an almighty effort, before I put her in the chance of becoming a mother. I did what that fellow Onan, or Hodad or something did in the Bible – let my seed scatter on the ground without wondering too much whether or not the grass was grateful. Holly lay there in the shade looking at me out of her horizon-blue eyes from which were squeezing big tear drops. A dark trickle of blood creased her legs – high up. There was a lump in my throat as big as a golf ball. I stroked her damp wave of honey-coloured hair back from her forehead.

"I'm not going to apologize. I've been wanting to do that ever since I first laid eyes on you. You – you – oh, dammit. . . ."

Holly got to her feet and examined the ruins of her white dress.

"There's nothing to apologize for, Danny," she said in a strange, quiet little tone. "I'm as much to blame as you – maybe more. But then – then I wanted it too, I guess." She turned her head away to hide the tears.

"At least you won't be in the family way."

"And what if I was?" she said fiercely. "I wouldn't ask you to marry me. Just because I happen to be one of the Wild Dallans and an easy push-over doesn't mean I don't have some pride.

"No, you wouldn't need to worry. You could go on seeing your high-class school teacher. I suppose you think I haven't heard all about how you used to meet her every Saturday and go wandering off into the trees with her. I just bet you did the same thing with her, Danny Mulcahy." Holly turned on me, stamping her foot.

"Tell me – was I just as good going as your fancy-pantied little Miss Warren? *Ohhhhhh!*" She scooped up her basket and jug and fled up the steep rocks toward her home. As she did, a tongue of chain lightning slid out of a high bank of ink-black clouds that had rolled up unnoticed by us. For an instant, Holly was limned in the glare, then she was swallowed up by the storm and a crack of thunder that made the ground tremble and set the horses to tugging uneasily at their halter shanks.

NINE

The haying was finished by the end of July. We folded our camp and left. Since that day of storm and other turbulences I hadn't met Holly nor, except for fleeting glances of her and some of the younger children picking huckleberries on the far ridges, had I seen her. When I did spot her, with her lard pail and berry sweep, she wasn't wearing her white dress. Twice, before the haying ended, I rode up to Holly's house by evening time, hoping to see her; but while the dogs and kids were as enthusiastically noisy in their greeting as ever and the old folks seemed genuinely glad of my company, of Holly there was no sign.

Life around the home place went on pretty much as usual. We shipped a carload of cattle, driving them to the stock-pens on the Canadian National siding at Riverdale. We put in a solid three days de-horning some two-year-old stuff, which was accomplished by driving them into a chute ending in a kind of box corral where the beeves could be caught and held. A de-horning tool was built on the same principle as a huge pair of pruning shears. The cutters were locked over the horns and the long handles closed, the knives slicing through horn and cartilage easily enough. There was a fair amount of blood and bawling and spraying of grass-green cow-blubber, so I was relieved when the job was done.

Well on in August, Uncle Mick and I drove into Riverdale. He had business at the bank and I killed some time at Klausen's Clothing Emporium, arguing with the clerk and the tailor about the cloth, fit and cut of a new suit I was designing to buy. Knowing next to nothing about the tailoring profession, I came into the argument unhampered by any great accumulation of facts and I had to resort to the technique of "not knowing anything about art, but knowing what I liked." Although I wasn't aware of it at the time, I have since learned that haberdashery clerks in small centres such as Riverdale are just about the vilest examples of low sartorial accomplishment you could meet within a day's gallop. I walked in from the street wearing what I thought was a reasonably decent rig-out; what it lacked in style it made up for in comfort: a soft, pearl-grey flannel shirt tucked into a well-scrubbed pair of Lee denims and a set of high-topped, flat-heeled riding boots. I don't suppose a general shirt and tie shop of the class of Klausen's *(Caps for Dad and His Lad)* catered to a clientele more discriminating than, say, the station agent or the new teller at the Imperial Bank, who had been sent to Riverdale from Oshawa and therefore knew by instinct that purple arm-garters were out and the metal expanding kind were in. Yet Klausen and his clerk acted as if they customarily fitted and suited Douglas Fairbanks or Mr. Jimmy Walker, who had been the natty mayor of New York City. We came to terms on a dark blue, single-breasted cut with a running pin stripe of quiet red and white. I resisted all efforts of the staff to unload upon me a batch of four-in-hand ties. I did buy a couple of white shirts with soft, turn-down

110

collars. I've never seen the essential use of a neck-tie, either functional or ornamental.

The suit I'd picked off the rack had to be left for alterations, so I stuck my thumbs in my belt loops and wandered out on the street to take in the entertainment Riverdale might offer on a hot August afternoon. Except for Matt Kavanagh sweeping the sidewalk in front of his general store and the occasional racing of a car motor over in Blaine's garage, I could have seen and heard more action in the piney woods back at the ranch. A high-topped old Model T Ford with a brass radiator and calcium carbide lights was parked at the curb in front of Dolan's Fancy Meats & Sausages. As I sauntered by I saw Holly Dallan sitting in the passenger side of the front seat trying very hard not to look at me. She sat stiff as a tamarack pole, in a checked dress that had puffed sleeves and a pile of ruffing around the neck. It may have been an attractive gown for a woman of fifty on her way to a church social. Holly had her hair pulled back and tied with a red ribbon. I planted a foot on the running board.

"Hello Holly."

"Hello." She gazed straight down the street as if there was something supremely interesting in the order of a circus parade passing across her line of sight. I tweaked at her hair ribbon.

"Look – why are you so uppity-nosed? I tried to see you – afterward – and you made quite a point of keeping yourself scarce. I've wanted to see you. I'd like to take you to the Orange Hall Saturday night – there's a travelling show coming: The Swiss Bell Ringers. . . ."

She turned a soft, cloudy look on me.

"I thought you would be ashamed of me."

"Balls I am! . . . I mean, like heck I am." I opened the door. "Come on and have an ice-cream soda with me."

"Why – I – I don't know. . . ."

"I'd purely admire to take the prettiest girl in Longford for an ice-cream soda."

She got out of the car rather diffidently and put a timid hand in the crook of my arm. Her dress hung straight down to her calves. I liked it better when she wore short skirts. Put a sunbonnet on her and stand Holly alongside a covered wagon and a span of oxen, and you would have had a picture of an emigrant train heading for Oregon in the 1850's. Still, with her tawny hair and sky-blue eyes setting off her tanned features, she was a mighty pretty girl. I could sense the blood leaping through the veins of my arm at the touch of her fingers.

We went into the ice-cream parlour and took a table near the window so we had a clear view of the street and all the excitement going on. The table had twisted wire legs as had the chairs. The waitress was behind the counter reading a copy of the Lindsay *Post* which, when we came in, she put aside and pretended to act bored, stifling a fair imitation of a yawn. She stood by, tapping her pencil against the order pad; she looked at Holly as if such extremities of dress shouldn't, by common law, be allowed, but with the air that serving all sorts of oddments was her job and she couldn't be held accountable for whatever trade drifted in off the street.

Holly studied the menu as if it was the Old Testament written entirely in Chinese. She said she guessed she'd have a soda.

"What kinda soda did 'ja want? we got strawberry, vanilla 'n coffee flavour."

I saw the waitress's game and cut right through it.

"We'll have coffee-flavoured," and, just in case she was wondering if we were good for the bill, I spun a big, shiny American silver dollar on the marble table. The waitress patted the back of her hair and arched a hip out; she let me have a wide smile that would have been brilliant except her teeth were dirty.

Little by little Holly was softening; once her knee touched mine, sending an electrical charge clean through me. She tackled her soda with the delight of a kid, scraping the last bit out with her spoon and licking her lips.

"About going with you on Saturday night – I don't know; I'll have to ask Paw. . . ."

"I'll ask him. Right today. I would have, anyway."

Holly looked at me as if I were Sir Lancelot of the Lake and Buffalo Bill Cody rolled into one. At that point, my uncle strolled in, looking big and easily handsome in a straw skimmer and a white shirt with the sleeves rolled above the elbow showing arms the size of stovepipes. He raised his hat to the waitress and gave her the benefit of his gold teeth.

"Good afternoon, Grace – pretty as ever, I see. Just bring me a beaker of ginger ale with a lump of ice – thank you."

He slid his bulk into our table, tossed his hat cleverly on a wall hook and folded his big arms.

"Miss Holly – this nephew of mine has the habit of finding the comeliest young ladies. I should have known better than to send him back to your dad's to cut hay. Did you, or did you not, promise me last summer that you were going to grow up and marry me? Now, here you are – all grown and easily the most attractive young woman in the County, saving," he said, with a sly dropping of his eyelids, "a certain school teacher whose merits are not to be denied."

Always, Mick had the ability to make me feel young, tender-footed and at a loss for words. And always I resented this to the point where I would get ready to cut loose at him when he would shift his tack and say or do something to draw the sting. Some refer to this as the innate Irish charm and others claim it to be pure Irish deviousness; I suspect, with Mick at least, it was a combination of both.

He reached over with a big hand and covered Holly's slim brown fingers. Mick's hands were muscular, covered with short, strong, dark hairs; the nails were flat, broad and well-groomed.

"There are posters about announcing an entertainment Saturday night. If Danny doesn't quickly ask for your company at this gala, I will. Of course, if he does ask you and if you consent, I shall feel obliged to loan him the car, otherwise he might take it into his head to have you lead Gertie while he rides. Danny, you see, is from the out-backs of Alberta and unfamiliar with the civilised customs of Brulé and Longford."

He rose, made a graceful bow in Holly's direction and strolled away.

"He's such a nice man," Holly breathed, "but I don't always know what to make of him."

"He's a long-winded old yahoo," I grumbled, half-proudly, "and don't go trying to make anything more of him than he's already done for himself. I was going to ask him about the car. Sometimes I think he knows what's going to happen three days ahead of time."

When we got back to the Ford, Holly's old man was behind the wheel waiting for her.

"Jeezus christ an' the calves got out! I thought you'd gone for a leak and walked clear down the railroad tracks to have it. Get in, we gotta get goin'. Say, Danny – d'yuh mind windin' up the auty fer us?"

I went around to the front of the Ford, shoved in the hand crank against its spring until it engaged and was set to turn the motor over, when Cully stuck his head out.

"I got her spark retarded far's she'll fuckin' well go, but watch her or she'll back-burl 'n kick the nuts off you."

A town lady with a parasol spread to stand off the sun stopped in her tracks at the sound of this Longford English, or maybe she wanted to have a ringside seat when somebody was having his nuts kicked off by a 1914 Ford. Conscious that I was being watched, especially by Holly, I bulged my shoulder muscles and spun the crank. The motor coughed, caught fire, and the Dallans clattered away, Holly waving frantically to me as they made a U-turn and headed for the north rocks.

Now a young fellow may be of two minds about a girl – what the educated folk refer to as ambivalence. I had this double feeling about Elaine and I sure enough had it for Holly. Now I calculated Elaine to be just about the nicest, loveliest piece of woman flesh I'd ever laid eyes on; at the same time it didn't stop me from trying to put a hand on her pretty legs just due south of where her shorts ended. And my feeling for Holly sure hadn't got in the way of going a whole lot further. After the episode under the white oak back at the beaver meadows, I felt like kicking myself for taking advantage of a girl I'd esteemed to have shucked her pants several times around the circuit only to find she was as virginal as a spring lamb. This desire to self-kick was being eased out of rank by the urge to try it all over again when I remembered the way her hand burned on my arm and how the front of her gingham dress swelled out. I wasn't exactly green about some rudimentary principles; with those in mind, I headed for Stimson's drug

114

store, figuring that to be fore-armed is as good as thrice-warned.

The druggist was hanging onto the wall phone when I entered. He nodded at me and continued speaking to the mouthpiece in a whine like a dog begging at the back door to be let in out of the cold.

"Yes, Missus O'Connor. Yes, I have. I can recommend Ayer's Cherry Pectoral. Oh he did? Doc Armbruster say that, did he? Well, I've some new tonic in just this week: Broadbent's Eclectic Bitters. Yup. Yup. Three tablespoons daily after meals . . . I'll be right with you, young fellow. . . . Yup. I'll send it out with Ed Flynn – saw him around town a minute ago; he'll be goin' out your way. Yup. Good-bye.

"And now what can I do for you, young fellow my lad?"

I was about to order a tin of Sheiks or maybe Golden Phoenix or some other kind of rubber condom, when the woman with the parasol came in and I braked to a halt and did a smart about-turn.

"Do you have a box of candy that would be nice for a girl?" An idiot's way of putting it – a fellow would hardly want a box of candy that would be nice for a horse.

Stimson dived into a glass show-case and came up with a box of chocolates coloured a violent purple and tied up with a bandage of yellow ribbon. Parts of the box had a faded look where the sun had got at it. I paid for it and fled.

On the Friday of that week, I rode to Horncastle to pick up any mail. Rilance said there wasn't any, but he retrieved a folded piece of paper from our pigeon-hole and handed it to me.

"Here – that Dallan girl – the one they call Holly left this here for you. Just left it here and said to give it to you. I'm supposed to be running a post office here, not a messenger service. You'd think a 3¢ stamp wouldn't be beyond the reach of even the Dallans."

"You'll get it back the next time you weigh your thumb along with the dog meat you pass off as baloney," I answered.

I took the note outside so the storekeeper wouldn't be tempted to look over my shoulder. It was lined paper like that used in school copy books and the message was in pencil:

Dear Danny,
You forgot to ask Paw if I could go
Saturday night. I asked him and I can.
I will wear my white dress, the one you
like.

love
Holly
XXXXXX

I sent Gertie into a wild run down the road, waving my hat grandly at Mrs. Charlie George and giving my version of a rebel yell as I passed. She must have thought Quantrill and his gang were raiding Horncastle.

After supper the next day, I shaved carefully, searching for whiskers that weren't there and wishing I had an iron stubble like Uncle Mick's. I splashed on a half-pint of Yardley's lotion, gave a last flick of my handkerchief over my oxfords that were sitting gleaming on a chair and put on the suit and shirt Mick had picked up in Klausen's the day before. It fitted about as well as could be expected and I spent a few minutes admiring the cut of myself in the yellowing mirror above the kitchen sink.

With the candy box under my arm I went out to the Plymouth; I had spent the best part of the day washing and grooming it. The nickeled headlights gleamed. I had even curried the bumpers and shined the tail light. Mick came through the gate; he had walked over to the store a couple of hours before. He walked slowly, as if his bursitis was acting up.

"Danny. . . ." He wasn't looking at me, but at a point somewhere past my shoulder. I had never seen him at a loss for words before.

"Danny – Holly slipped off the bridge on her way home from the post office, yesterday. She must have struck her head on a rock when she tumbled in the river. They found her body three miles down the Black this morning."

The sun turned black. There was a roaring in my ears like the crashing of waves on an ocean shore. My uncle was saying something but I couldn't hear what he said.

I dropped the box of candy and slowly, methodically set my

116

foot on it and tramped it to obliteration under my newly-polished shoes.

Later, when Mick had poured two tumblersful of raw whiskey into me, I looked up at him, removing my gaze from the kitchen table I had been staring at for an hour.

"But she was as sure-footed as a deer; she wouldn't miss her step."

Mick was standing, staring out of the window, his back broad and dark against the fading light. He didn't turn around, but his voice was gentle.

"Perhaps her eyes were on a cloud."

I started to cry, then – but no tears came – just hard, tearing sobs that griped my stomach. From that day to this I've never cried again.

They waked Holly Dallan in the parlour of the log house where she had been born and reared. Charlie Bass, the undertaker, had smoothed over the gash on her temple. She was in her white dress; in her hands, folded across her breast, was the spray of lady's-slippers I picked in the bog for her. I remembered she had told me she loved lady's-slippers. She seemed small and fragile lying there in the plain pine coffin.

When Mick and I arrived on Sunday afternoon, a steady rain was slanting out of the northeast; low-scudding clouds, dark fringed and trailing raggedy edges, moved steadily across the sweep of granite now turned slick and sienna under the lash of rain. For once, no children came boiling into the yard to greet strangers; even the blue-ticks were morosely silent, lying under their accustomed tree wet and disconsolate. A few autos and horse-drawn rigs were drawn up in the yard.

Trudy Dallan may have been an ignorant woman of the back-rock districts; she may have been all that George Heeney made her out to be, but there was dignity and intuitiveness to the woman I've found lacking in many a higher-born, better-positioned lady. While my uncle stopped in the kitchen, shaking hands with Cully and the older boys in turn, Mrs. Dallan shooed a few people out of the parlour.

She squeezed my hand hard. "You'll want to be alone with

Holly for a few minutes."

As long as I live and struggle for breath I will never forget that scene: the poor drab parlour with bare, painted pine floors, the dark, rusty curtains shrouding the single window, the faded wallpaper with smears of hair grease at head level above an old sofa the colour of a dead rhinoceros. I had given the mother my spray of flowers, lady's-slippers wrapped in sphagnum moss to preserve their freshness; these she tucked gently between her daughter's folded hands. The coffin was set upon two saw trestles by the window and there the dead girl lay. I placed my two hands on hers and kneeled, leaning my head against her coffin. I didn't cry. My crying was done forever.

I was sixteen years old and had lost three people I had loved. The soul of the boy took wings and fled; the soul of man, scarred and bleeding, entered.

A tiny Bethel church and burying-ground, east along the road that led to the hamlet of Northmore, was where we interred Holly Dallan. I helped shoulder her coffin into the church, hearing not a word the Fundamentalist preacher blabbered about resurrection and death and life eternal safe within the arms of the Lord.

When all had gone, save my uncle and the two gravediggers and myself, I stood bare-headed in the still-falling rain while the red sand fell shovel by shovel onto the rough box, until the soil was mounded and patted above her final home. Beyond the pines I heard the mutter of the river that had robbed her of life. Never again could I take any pleasure from that river, nor would I consent to cut beaver hay there again.

One of the gravediggers was the pulp-faced young fellow that had snickered at me the night Doris Rilance and I went to the crokinole party. When the burial was complete he pulled a flask of cheap white wine from his raincoat and offered me a drink. He laughed coarsely.

"Too bad," he grinned, showing gapped, ugly teeth. "I bet that little floozy would have made a great piece of straddling."

I hit him. I hit him so hard his feet flew out from a red mask where I had broken his nose.

"If you ever cross my sight I'm going to kill you. I'm going to take a gun and shoot you in the belly and watch you die like the crawling reptile you are."

He made as if to grab a shovel and get up; Mick kicked it out of his hand and set his foot on his throat.

"Don't let the sun set on you another day in this part of the country," Mick grated. "I am going to come looking for you; I don't wish to find you."

Later I heard that black bastard caught a train to Haileybury in the north part of the province. He may not have been scared of my threat; he knew better than to disregard Michael Mulcahy.

TEN

By mid-August, the summer hung over Brulé like a wet cloth gone sour from too many applications to the head of a feverish person. The sun got up in the morning and went to bed at night without once taking a rest from the business of scorching the earth by ducking behind a cloud. The water-holes shrank to pots of scum in the centre of mud-wallows pocked and holed where the cattle laboured to their hocks to get at the blood-warm ooze in the centre. Perch Creek had shrunk to a runnel ghosting without a murmur through arum and pickerelweed. Even the Culm subsided to a sluggish grumping; the dark water stank of bacterial mud and reeking fish. Those sections of the pastures with skins stretched close to the underlying shale turned seed-brown and writhed beneath the glare of the sun. The stock drowsed all day in the deep shade of the maples, feeding at cool of dusk and dawn. The purgatorial climate affected Uncle Mick so badly he even slung a hammock between two of the Lombardy poplars, sleeping in it in preference to his shake-down on the old leather sofa in the kitchen. He never, to my knowledge, slept in one of the upstairs bedrooms, although he kept his clothing and an assortment of gear in one of the north rooms that had a window looking over the creek.

One Sunday morning, he was shaving while I was whaling into a plate of wheat-cakes and bacon and reading *Two Years Before the Mast*. Mick used a straight razor with unforgivable deftness; by way of emulation I tried my burgeoning whiskers with the same weapon and came very near losing the lower end of an ear.

"Go and take a dip in what remains of the creek," Mick advised, sponging off remnants of lather from his face. He was bare to the waist; except for the mass of iron-grey hair on his chest that looked like a mound of steel wool, he had the torso of a young prize-fighter.

"I had a bath in the river last night, if it's any of your business. Anyway, we sleep far enough apart so you can hardly smell me. Why all this rush for cleanliness?"

"You shouldn't wait until your scent carries clear to George Heeney's. At any rate, I wasn't suggesting you stank. I'm paying a social call on people of some refinement – the Stackpoles. Clifford and I were in college together. He majored in economics and the higher algebra. He went all the way to the top, did Clifford; he is now the County Treasurer, with a brick residence in Riverdale, a wife who sings contralto, and a niece who is, without doubt, the homeliest female north of the Scugog River, not excepting the fair Tanglefoot. . . .

"Which reminds me – did you know that Toot Finnerty is apt to receive seven years free bread and water? But I want you to meet the Stackpole niece. She has no looks, has a remark-ably deficient figure and lays claim to no talents whatsoever. She will be good for you – even you can feel superior in her company."

The Stackpoles were everything Mick said they were and worse. They lived in the south part of Riverdale, which is to say, the best part. A small lake known as Fishtu Lake lay south and east of the town; the best houses had a clear view of the lake, a view bought at the expense of chopping down every tree along the waterfront, gouging out the stumps and flattening what was left with rolling equipment. I asked Mick the howcome of a name like Fishtu for a lake. He said the old Indian name for it was Onnonanhirsutis which, in Indian, meant hairy penis. When the first white man drifted along, the Indian chief went to tell him the name of the lake, but sneezed instead; the talk drifted on to something else and the white man just assumed the name was Fishtu. Later on, the County Historical Society argued about the origins of the name and they finally decided it came from an Indian name meaning "Laughing Girl Water." Mick said if historians could turn a sneeze into something like that he wondered what they might have done with a three-alarm fart.

The Stackpole house was of red brick; it sat two-storied square with a portico and colonnades in front, and a screened verandah at the back so they could sit there in the summer and examine the beauties of Fishtu without having to tussle the mosquitoes. There were the standard peony clumps, bleeding heart, cabbage roses and a garage with a brand new Marquette inside.

Clifford Stackpole may have had a degree from the University of Toronto, but he hadn't allowed it to affect his mind. He had a long, thin, money-grubber's nose and slate-coloured eyes that examined the world closely and coldly from behind gold-rimmed spectacles. He combed what was left of his hair in thin strands across his scalp, and talked knowingly of mortgages and dividends and debentures that periodically either floated or sank, with one hand rammed into his side pocket and his foot lapping over his knee. He wore a grey suit, a ginger-coloured tie and a high collar that was the going thing about 1905. His boots were above the ankle and had elastic sides.

We sat in the parlour, dismal and brown from too much walnut and not enough air. Generations of dead and buried Stackpoles glared down from behind walnut rings spaced along the walls. Mrs. Stackpole, a bosomy woman of sixty or so and with her hair washed in a blue rinse that gave her the appearance of

122

a moulting polar-bear, served sherry in tiny goblets, and wafer-biscuits on a silver plate.

"Daniel," she said, smiling at Mick, "might enjoy lemonade and a cookie."

"Daniel would indeed enjoy a lemonade and a cookie," my uncle replied gravely. "The young rascal has raided a couple of cookie-jars back around Horncastle."

While each was sipping his own and I gnawed at a cookie that had a dead raisin in the middle of it, old Stackpole beamed at his wife.

"Ethel – can we persuade you to do one of your numbers for us. I am sure Michael would enjoy something other than this modern jazz sop one hears on the radio." He turned around and beamed at Mick.

"I was remarking to Daniel on the way out," Mick lied, "that I hoped Mrs. Stackpole would be in voice today. By all means, do favour us."

Mrs. Stackpole simpered and perched before the piano. She scratched around through some sheet music, pounced out a trial note or two on the keyboard, and then flung herself into "What Are the Wild Waves Saying." She had a voice that was full of soarings, tremolos, quaverings and up-draughts. At the end I still didn't know what those wild waves had said and I didn't get to find out because the last note was still shaking Grandpaw Stackpole in his frame above the piano when the niece came in, squatted ungracefully on a chair and yanked her skirt down over her red, chapped knees. All of her skin had a red, chapped look – like a lobster that had been half-boiled. She had a startled, thyroid eye in her head; you can see that kind of eye in a skittery horse; in fact, if she'd been a horse you wouldn't have bought her.

Her name was Minerva.

An arrangement was made whereby Minerva was to show me the summer house that was at the end of a row of chinese-elm bushes between the house and the lake. While I was taken on this guided tour, the older folk came out and sipped their sherries on the verandah in case Minerva took it into her head to show me sights more wonderful than the summer house, which wasn't a hell of a lot when you came to examine it. It was made of lathes and had rambler roses, now just about beat for the season, crawling around inside and out. Minerva said she loved to come here and commune with the gods and muses and read all of the poetry of Pauline Johnson. She had mottled teeth and the smile of a lynx.

At dinner I had to sit beside Minerva and endure her twaddle and eat dried roast beef and dried boiled cabbage and chomp dried ends of celery stuffed with god-knows-what but it stunk worse than George Heeney's feet.

Stackpole was chanting his own praises; judging from the ease with which he worked his way through the script, I assumed he had travelled the same route many times before. Then he turned on me, giving me the benefit of his sixty-five years of penny-pinching and nickel-grubbing.

"*Yaaai-ss,* you young fellows of today don't know the meaning of work." He had a nasal voice halfway between a whinner and a whine. "I still put in my twelve hours. If I were you, my boy, I'd be into mathematics – solid numbers and solid figuring. Figures don't lie. You can trust a figure. Get your numbers right and pretty soon you can start counting your dollars, right – Michael?"

"Daniel has already taken to studying forms and figures with remarkable acumen, although not always judiciously." Mick solemnly forked beef into his mouth.

Stackpole alternated between blowing the horn of his past and offering sound advice for my future all through the dessert, which was baked apples – dry, of course. Even the sauce managed to come out dry. I never liked baked apples, although I took a spoonful more or less out of politeness – a gesture that got me no place because Stackpole put it all down to orneriness.

"I'd have thought a good home-cooked meal would have been more than welcome after bachelor beans and hardtack. Minerva worked the better part of an hour on that dessert . . . Baked Alaska is her pride and joy," he complained.

I figured I'd had about all the sheep-dip I was obliged to take and that it was time for the worm to turn and tear a strip off the robin.

"If Minerva wants to bake Alaska and pan-fry the Yukon Territories while she's at it, that's her affair; but if this is a sample of her pride and joy maybe she'd be better off at harness-making. We may be bachelors, but I'd rather eat beans and hardtack and listen to the creek run than gnaw a roast from a seven-year-old bull and listen to you run." I crossed my knife and fork with deliberation on the remains of the apples.

The silence was ruinous. Minerva's red blotches ran into the white ones and the white ones shifted over to where the red usually hung out. I took a quick look at Mick, half expecting a crunch on the ear. In fact, everyone was looking at my uncle. He calmly finished his dessert.

"I liked your Baked Alaska, Minerva," he said, giving her one of those black-lashed blue-eyed looks that melted females into a state of gibbering compliancies. "Danny doesn't and he told you so. Clifford – you've become too accustomed to the adulation of ward-heelers and bootlickers. You confuse honesty with the ability to settle obligations. Your father was the main wheel of Stackpole & Drury. You didn't work as hard to get to where you believe you are, as you did to stay where your father started you from. This is, no doubt, admirable. At the same time, you could not have endured what Danny has endured of late without cracking straight down the middle. I've enjoyed your company and your dinner. I hope to do so again. But you might keep your urge to proselytize chained up. It never worked with me and, as you can see, it won't work with Danny."

A long, blue cigar-shaped cloud hung in the sky to the west where the sun had disappeared. Mick forged the Plymouth steadily through the peat marshes on either side of the road.

"You can't blame Clifford too much," he argued. "You can't fault him for being born into money and continuing the tradition. Without money he would be another George Heeney. Still – I wonder what possesses a man to build a mansion by a lake and then never really see the view. Perhaps that is Clifford's essential weakness – he was so preoccupied with building his concept of the good life he had no time for the view."

"How about your life – did you get to see the view?"

He nodded toward the west. "Sheet lightning over there; be a storm before midnight.

"Yes, I believe so. I was born in – let's see – 1866: the year before Confederation and the year after the American Civil War. We came to Canada in 1868. I am Irish by birth rather than inclination. My mother was of Anglo-Irish stock – Castle Irish the peasantry dubbed them. Her father was titled: Sir Arthur Neale. The Neales owned some property in Mayo. Father was in turn, stable-boy, hostler and trainer for the Neale stables.

"I rather think my mother – Penelope – fell in love with father and he fell in love with the idea of marrying into an aristocratic situation. Sir Arthur found out, of course, and threatened to remove Penelope to England. Father countered by promising to have the Fenians burn Rookeneale Manor to the foundation stones.

"Father won the bluff. At any rate, Sir Arthur had three other daughters so I presume he felt he could spare one. Father and mother were married in 1860 in two separate ceremonies – one Catholic and the other Anglican, or Church of Ireland, if you will. After a decent interval – ten months – Rosie was born, then John, then I.

"As long as mother was alive the Neales provided a measure of patronage for father and his family. When mother passed away, Sir Arthur gave the old man passage money and a ticket of good riddance covering him and all his issue from thence to thus.

"It seems to me that the native Irish are a race of flamboyant non-entities. Father was no exception. If the Celtic breed and seed of Ireland have produced a philosopher, an outstanding composer, a truly great poet, a unique literature or, God help us, even one passable military leader, I haven't heard of it."

I squirmed uneasily. I remembered my father bragging on the Irish although he had never set foot on the island and knew little enough of the people except what he'd heard or imagined. Elaine had taught me something of a group called the Irish Movement, although the only individual I could recall was somebody called Yeats.

"Well, this Yeats fellow is a first-rate poet and he's Irish."

"Anglo-Irish," Mick corrected. "Shaw, Synge, Stephens.

126

... All Anglo-Irish. The only thing I got out of being Irish was a dedication to the national occupational hazard – whiskey."

A brief flare of lightning scuttled across the sky – low and far away. It lit, for a moment, my uncle's face: dark and sad and shadowed with melancholy.

We sat out on the back porch watching the storm grumbling its way across the Longford Rocks and picking on down the Culm toward us. Mick hit a thoughtful lick on the banjo strings.

> I can't hear the thunder,
> I can't feel the rain;
> Away down in this prison. . . .

A fork of lightning sliced at the swaying crowns of the pines standing along the river. I wished my uncle could leave his prison, although I wasn't sure what that prison was or what the bars and cells were made from. But the glare of the lightning threw the shadow of the vine trellis so that bars slanted across his face and striped his white shirt in the way a member of a chain gang had striped clothing. I wanted to put out my hand and touch him on the shoulder and tell him we were partners in loneliness, but nothing lasted forever. Then he changed the chord, whanging the banjo free and open in the manner they call "cobblestoning."

> Did you ever see Nellie make water?
> She pisses a beautiful stream –
> It runs for a mile and a quarter
> And you can't see her arse for the steam.

And that was Uncle Mick all over: just when you thought you were getting to know him and wanted to reach out and make common feeling with him, he veered off and changed direction, letting the curtains close about his eyes so that you didn't know any more about what he thought or how he felt than you did to begin with.

127

ELEVEN

The last week of August was as hot as the first. The electric storm had cooled nothing. What it had done was blow a shutter off the library window. This set me to examining the other shutters which I found rusted fast to their anchor bolts and rotting in several places from pure lack of attention. On a Tuesday evening when I knew the store would be open, I rode Gertie over to Horncastle to buy an assortment of nails I would need to tackle the shutter renovations.

Ed Rilance, his wife, Doris, George Heeney and Charlie George were sitting in a group on the concrete floor of the verandah, pawing lazily at night-fliers and listening to Ed hold forth on glories past. His subject tonight was Tanglefoot.

"She was a Briscoe. Em' Briscoe's girl. He had three of 'em

128

but one got drownded and a steer stepped on the other'n when she was a toddler; you could see the outline of the hoof print right on her head – high up on the side it was – when she was laid out. Pericles Bass was alive then and Charlie was learnin' the business. It was a county funeral so Pericles sent Charlie to do the layin' out. He didn't know whether to fill the hole the hoof had made with putty and bung her over and file her smooth, or let her lay. He let her lay."

Heeney grunted and spat a quart of tobacco juice between his feet.

"I mind that. Em' went to Cliff Stackpole who was reeve at the time. Stackpole goes to Pericles an' says, 'What you charge fer a kid's coffin?' Pericles says, 'They's two kinds: oak 'n basswood. Basswood's cheapest – five dollars.' Stackpole says, 'This here's public funds we're foolin' around with. Get an orange crate and line it with a pillow or somethin' – and charge the county a buck.' And by the sweet powers of Christ that's what they buried her in. I know when they went to heave the box in the back of the hearse one of the slats pulled off and the kid damn near rolled out. Say that musta been thirty years ago. . . ."

"Twenty-seven," corrected Rilance. "It was in 19 ought and 4. The reason I know was that was the year Charlie here, shingled his house. I heard about it from Cully Dallan. He was courtin' Cackling Jack Jowett's girl over near Slab Town and he come by and told me Em' Briscoe's kid was done up. I remember I went over to tell Charlie and he was shinglin' the south side; he had about seven or eight courses laid. Bought the shingles from Ike Broom, didn't you, Charlie?"

"Nope. Jimmy McCandy." Charlie wasn't long on discussion.

"*Hmmm.* I could have sworn you bought from Broom." Rilance looked aggrieved.

I was somewhat surprised to see Mrs. Rilance. In the several months since I had come to live in Brulé I hadn't seen the woman out and about more than twice. She looked like her daughter was going to look give her another twenty-five years: the same prominent thighs and wet brown eyes with thick glasses. Doris sat in a rocker, knees slightly splayed, a curious smile on her

129

face like the smile on a painting of a woman I saw once by some Italian painter.

After her father had traced the Briscoe line back to the first cat-house in these parts and had recited the names, sex and family tree of the four hearse horses that hauled away the orange-crated remains of the Briscoe infant, Doris rose and said there was a letter for me. That was a puzzle; I couldn't think of anyone who would be writing to me. Doris ducked in the store, went behind the wicket and fetched out a fragile envelope that she held at arm's length by the tips of her fingers. I looked at the neat, slanted writing on the back. It said: From Miss Elaine Warren, 119 Hobson Blvd., St. Catharines, Ont. I felt my face growing hot; I tucked the letter in my hip pocket, trying to look off-handed as if it was just a circular from an insurance company, but I didn't fool Doris a mite nor iota.

"*Veree* delicate perfume," she murmured.

I hadn't forgotten her treatment of me when the drummer had been in the store.

"I misdoubt you could buy the like of it in Horncastle."

Doris sniffed and turned her head. I chuckled inside and concluded the score to be even.

Elaine's letter, which I read at least five times by the light of the single bulb in the kitchen, went as follows:

My dear Danny: I truly apologize for not having written to you long before this, but the frank truth is I've spent the summer writing for my Master's degree. Even so, many teachers with PhD's are begging for jobs so I am pleased that my contract for another year has been approved by the powers-that-be on the 10th Concession of Brulé school-board. Could it be that your uncle had a fine Irish hand in all this? I realize I have no business, after my neglect of you, asking favours, but could you possibly meet my train at Beaverton on August 30th? It is due to arrive in Beaverton about 8.30 pm. Oh Danny – it will be truly wonderful to see you again and go for walks and have study sessions with you. It would be just my luck to come back and find that you have met a perfectly charming girl and have forgotten poor me. I hope not. Please write as soon as possible or telephone me collect. My number is at the bottom of the page. All my love to you and my warmest regards to Mr. Mulcahy.

Elaine.

Mick was studiously avoiding any notice of me and my letter; he had on his reading glasses and made out to be heavily concentrating on his book.

"What are you reading?" I asked. "Oh – Pope's 'Rape of the Lock.' I heard about that."

Mick elevated his eyebrows. "Have you heard of Locke's 'Rape of the Pope'?"

"Here's a letter from the school ma'am." I tossed it carelessly in front of him.

"Well," Mick remarked, "I would be tempted to loan you the car provided she had sent me her love and you her warmest regards. I see little profit in spending money on gas for warm regards; I'd do much more for love."

I was at the station by eight o'clock, waiting impatiently for the Toronto train to pull in. The Plymouth had been washed and curried. I'd even bought a kind of sachet rig to hang inside and provide a perfume which if it failed to overpower the fragrance of cow manure, would at least balance it.

The wind had switched to the northeast, bringing a steady slanting rain from low-tumbling clouds; there was a sense of autumn in the air. I pulled up the collar of my slicker and watched the rain fall on the shiny rails.

Elaine climbed down from the day coach lugging a pair of suitcases; I ran and grabbed both of them and stowed them in the car while she chattered at me. She was wearing a dark green suit and a hat with a perky feather.

"You better get in before your hat starts to moult." I held the door open, grinning at her.

"I'm dying for a cup of coffee and a sandwich. I'm sure the

Garritys will be snug in their trundle beds by the time we get there and I will be faced with the prospect of luke-warm tea at breakfast."

"Let's explore Beaverton until we find a restaurant." I turned the car toward the main section of the town.

Elaine's tongue wagged as fast as the flap on a duck's fanny while we had coffee and raisin pie. Some of the news I could have done without. She had met this wonderful man – a teacher like herself. He was so cultured and so travelled and so debonair.

"Well, he's already three things that I ain't," I declared. "Was you to keep going you could probably run the score up to ten or eleven."

Elaine giggled.

"I do believe you're jealous."

"I am in a pig's ass!"

It was out before I could bite my tongue, but if Elaine was shocked she didn't let on.

On the drive back she snuggled up close to me. The rain made a comfortable, satisfying sound on the roof; the windshield wipers clashed back and forth while growing puddles spread themselves before the headlights.

When we drove in through Garrity's gate, we could see all the lights were out and the house was as dark as a funeral parlour on Hallowe'en night. While I pulled her luggage out of the car Elaine tried the front door.

"Locked." She made a grimace. "And I wrote them over a week ago to tell them when I expected to be here."

I drove my boot-heel at the door until it threatened to part brass-rags from the hinges.

An upstairs window creaked open; Garrity's night-capped head poked out into the rain.

"Who's that? Cut that out! I'll come down there amongst yez in a minute."

"Come on, Rapunzel . . . let down your golden hair and I'll climb up it. Miss Warren would be pleased to come in out of the damp and the elements."

The night-cap recoiled and had a bit of a conflab with something else inside the building, then re-appeared.

"The key is under the mat, Miss Warren. I thought you knew.

Who is that with you? Is it that young bugger of a Mulcahy?"

"Pull in your head before it gets wet. I thought for a minute we'd fetched up at the cow-barn or the goat-shed when I heard you bleat."

Elaine hissed at me to hush up. I dug around under the mat and located the key. I carried her luggage inside. She kissed me quickly on the cheek and I was back out in the rain. Garrity was giving me the evil eye from his perch.

"Are you still there? have you your head caught? you might better open the window before you go poking your head out. At least the best part of you won't get cold."

I thumbed my nose at him and headed for home, still feeling the warm place on my cheek where Elaine's lips had brushed me.

For several weeks I was too busy to see much of Elaine. Uncle Mick divined that the cattle market probably would drop even lower, so we shipped eighty-odd head of mixed beeves to Toronto. A few days later the bottom fell out of beef prices and Mick went on a tour of the townships, buying weaned calves and feeder stock while they could be had cheaply. Meanwhile I had repaired the ailing shutters, brought in an electrician from Lindsay to add more wiring and outlets to the house and set about panelling the walls of the three ground-floor rooms. I fixed over the kitchen in pine, the parlour in birch and the library in oak. All this brought the wrath of Mick down on my head when he got the bills. Finally he admitted he was getting tired of looking at the same old wall-paper year in and day out, but he advised me to consult with him before I went ahead and laid in water pipes to hook up with Lindsay.

On a Saturday morning early in October, Mick was taking his ease on the front verandah while I filed a circular saw blade. The sumacs and sugar maples were flared out in scarlet and yellow and the bittersweet vines were a running fire of orangey-red among the hawthorn crowns.

"What is that dot of scarlet yonder?" Mick pointed. "I do believe the sumacs are on the march. It's Birnam Wood coming to Dunsinane."

I peered at the low range of hills toward the southwest.

"Looks like a woman. I think it's Elaine."

" 'Elaine' now, is it? We progress. I'm wondering what travail has brought her to Mulcahy Castle on such a fine morning?"

I went back to my filing, concentrating with such fine resolution on what I was doing, I filed only three teeth from the wrong angle. Mick was a third of his way through a flask of white wheat whiskey standing handy to one of his hairy paws on the verandah floor.

The teacher was steering a collision course straight for the house; when she came within hailing distance she waved cheerily. My heart thumped so loudly I was scared Mick would hear it and get to jeering. Elaine looked as bright as an autumn tree herself, in a red cape and a jaunty red tam-o-shanter with a perky feather stuck upright in it.

Mick was on his feet at her approach and bowing grandly, hat in one hand and the other stretched amiably toward the girl.

"Miss Warren – I – we – are delighted. I remarked to Danny no later than last night 'we must have Miss Warren over for tea.' But Danny insists always on work before pleasantries and he must file his saws and be about his labours, leaving his poor uncle to entertain as best he might."

"Mr. Mulcahy," Elaine laughed gaily, "you are the most charming liar I've ever met."

There was a nip in the air and we were all grateful for the pine fire I kindled in the range to set the coffee pot boiling, Elaine having turned down Mick's offer of whiskey. We sat at the table and I was glad I'd put a new red-checked oilcloth on a week before.

I was astonished when Elaine turned deliberately to my uncle and, sticking her firm little jaw out, said, "Mr. Mulcahy, I want you to send Danny to high school."

Mick's smile stayed, but his eyes shadowed.

"And does Danny so want?"

"I don't know – we've not discussed anything of the sort. But with his ability and eagerness to learn he should have a proper chance at a good education and perhaps university."

"And what then? . . ."

"Well, he could be almost anything – a doctor or a lawyer or any of the professions he chose."

134

Mick waved his hand toward the library.

"There is an entire university here at his beck and call. There is another out there." He gestured toward the hills shining red and gold through the windows. "If Danny wishes to be a professional man I have no objection. I am but his uncle, neither his guardian nor keeper. But before you decide within your pedagogue's soul to confine Danny to an office, to pavement, to the dreary ramblings of professors, ask yourself what he could better learn and benefit by at some temple of the higher education than he obtains here?

"Here," Mick went on, "Danny has learned something about cattle; he has worked with wood and tools; he can tell what tree grows where and what flower blooms when. He can identify the call of a bird and mark a hawk in flight."

"And maybe he's learned to drink whiskey and carouse at dives," the teacher said hotly.

Mick's face was haunted. "And that, too, although to my knowledge Danny's carousing has been minimal."

"If both of you are finished argufying over my proposed career maybe you'll let me decide for myself. I have. I'm staying if that's the way Uncle Mick wants it. It's his place and if he don't want me around all he has to do is say so.

"I don't know what brought all this education business up because I'm happy the way I am." I got up and rattled the coffee pot angrily on the stove.

The twin temper spots on either cheek washed away and Elaine smiled.

"I'm sorry. I am impulsive that way. It's just that I was lying awake last night thinking of Danny and how nice it would be for him to continue his schooling, so right after breakfast I marched right over here to work my iron will on both of you," she laughed, and the whole room rang with fairy bells.

It wasn't until later I got the significance of Elaine lying in bed awake and thinking of me, but I was almighty pleased to know she'd done so.

She stayed for lunch, helping with the dishes after Mick had rolled his cigarette and strolled outside to "look at the cattle." It seemed cosy and home-like to have Elaine fussing about in the kitchen and being womanly and clucking about the state of the garbage pail and attacking an ancient festoon of spider knots on the back porch.

"You know – we could do this all the time," I said, not looking at her.

She didn't answer.

I turned to face her and she was giving me a level look from those big green eyes. Her bosom rose and fell a little as though she had been running.

"What do you mean?"

"I just meant – well – maybe we could get married and keep house together regularly."

"Married?" she asked softly.

I nodded.

Elaine walked over and looked out the window where the Lombardy poplars were gone all golden brown like corn flakes.

"Oh yes, I'll be honest – I've thought of it. But you're young – so young; at least three years younger than I am. We'd have to wait, and you have so much living and learning ahead of you, as have I, for that matter.

"Oh Danny!" she wailed, collapsing onto a chair, "I don't know – I just don't know. I'm all torn and confused. I heard about that girl – Holly. And I was so horribly jealous I was almost glad she died. Isn't that perfectly awful? And you are bound to meet other girls – lots of them."

I pointed out that she hadn't been exactly standing still while she was on holiday – that she had met some well-groomed slicker that she'd spent the better part of half an hour describing to me in the restaurant in Beaverton.

Elaine smiled ruefully. "He was just a nothing – a nothing at all."

I was mightily relieved to hear that. I went and stood beside her chair, letting my fingers comb lightly through the waves of her hair. She stood up and clung to me and I kissed her hard until I could feel her teeth mashing into my lips.

While we were thus engaged, Mick returned, making a god-awful amount of noise – for him. He whistled and hummed and scraped his feet the last two hundreds yards.

Mick poured himself a healthy slug of whiskey, humming a whimmery kind of little tune as he did so.

136

"Miss Warren, I'm about to visit the dead. In point of fact – the late and reasonably lamented Frank Murphy, erstwhile farmer and one of the landed gentry. He is being waked this afternoon and far into the night. If you care to go along I shall be glad of your company. As for education, Danny shouldn't miss this; a wake is always an education, I've learned."

The three of us arrived at the Murphys' about nightfall. Elaine had decided that her raiment of the morning was hardly fit for a wake, so we elected to pick her up at Garrity's in the evening.

Frank Murphy was an ordinary kind of second-generation Irishman, being neither rich nor poor, simple nor profound. At the age of fifty-five or so he discovered a growth on his lower lip and, when the medical trades seemed unable to halt the spread, Murphy trotted off to the Martyrs' Shrine near Midland and climbed the stone steps on his knees praying as he climbed. When that didn't work, he went to Bracebridge to consult a lady healer whose stock in trade was the laying on of hands. Whatever she cured in Murphy, it wasn't the cancer eating away his lower face and that was why we were going to his wake.

The departed one had a widow, some grown children and odds and ends of relatives, some of whom had junketed from as far away as Detroit to see him safely on. One of these acted as usher and met us at the door. Murphy was laid out in state in a slate-grey coffin that must have cost three times as much as the family could afford. Seated around the casket were six ladies including the widow Murphy, all in black and heavily veiled as though they were a set of bee-keepers. As we filed in, the women set up a howling, rocking backwards and forth and clanking their rosaries while uttering the most dismal cries I've ever heard in my life.

We made a complete lap of the bier, I taking grim note of the cancer tracks that all of Charlie Bass's cosmetic arts had failed to cover on the dead man's face. This is what it boils down to, I thought. This is the end of the line and no turn-table and no switch and no reversing gears. Stretched out in his grey cubby for all time to come and four days beyond that was the mortal shell of Francis Alphonsus Murphy, son of the late Bridget and Jno. Murphy, who had married Eileen Mangan and lived happily ever afterward for upwards of thirty-odd years. His sole claim to fame everlasting was his election to the office of Faithful Navigator in the Knights of Columbus, St. Dominus Council. That and having the honour of passing the plate twice every Mass at the big brick Catholic church in Riverdale.

Now Frank Murphy lay still and cold and as grey as the fancy shell that enclosed him. His widow was one of those pale, tight-lipped Irish women whose natural viciousness was kept in check by a rigid system of keeping house whereby every sprint of lint and jot of dust was harried to hell and gone by a posse of brooms, mops and scrub-brushes. The Murphy house had the over-varnished smell of a church. The place was about as cozy as a cathedral.

After dropping to our knees long enough to mutter a few bars of the Rosary, we crossed ourselves – Elaine, being a Protestant, watched us covertly from her eye-corners so that she could follow suit – and after shaking the damp-handkerchiefed palm of Mrs. Murphy we traipsed awkwardly to the kitchen where a tall, angular woman with eyes like prune-pits was serving drinks and cutting cake. This was Adeline Murphy, the bachelor sister of Frank. She had the hand, foot and voice of a man; whether she had anything else about her that was masculine I can't say, and with her age and overall get-up there was nothing that would tempt anyone to scout around and find out.

"Well, Mike Mulcahy," she said in a booming voice, handing him a tumbler of raw whiskey, "that must be your nephew. Glad to see you, Miss Warren; how is the school these days?" She didn't wait for a reply, but jammed glasses and sandwiches into our hands.

"This is a sad time, Ad, a sad time." Mick found an empty chair and handed Elaine into it. I wished I could have thought a little faster on my feet instead of standing around looking dumb and feeling too big for the room and the dozen or so people that were in it.

"Sad for poor Frank," his sister replied. "But God, Michael, the man was dying by inches and knew it all the time. He said only last week when Father Devlin was here, 'Father,' he said, 'my time is short and I'll soon be with the saints and angels.' "

"How is Eileen taking it? She looks firm."

"That one!" Adeline tossed her head. "Sure, there's little enough that could rub the tarnish off her. Cold as brass, that woman, as was her mother before her. You remember Sally Mangan."

The Detroit member of the family came and called a short conference with the angular Miss Murphy and we joined the select company who were drinking Frank's whiskey, eating his provender and singing his praises mightily in return for their funereal suppers. In life, from what I had heard beforehand, Murphy was renowned for nothing in particular. He lacked the imagination to sin. But to hear the wakers at their trade you would think that the deceased was Giant MacCaskill, Paul Bunyan and Don Juan Quilligan all in one mighty body surpassed only by the profound intellect that governed every move, action and speech the dead man ever made while he was yet among us. The Irish have no particular affection for solemn accuracy and at wakes, or when recalling the past, the blinders are off and the horse runs free. One fellow, with a head like a goat and a gimpy leg he favoured by holding out to the kitchen fire, turning it from side to side as if he was roasting a hot-dog, went into a long verbal dance about the merits of Murphy that, if only a quarter true, would have qualified the possessor for canonization.

"Oh boys oh boys, I'm tellin' yus, there was not a man north of the Scugog or south of the Magnetawan that could follow Frank Murphy for a day's work. I seen him plough a furry that was as straight as a die so yus could be measurin' it with a surveyor's peep-glass."

"Was he pretty strong?" piped up a young fellow about my age.

"Strong?" said the speaker, turning his knee in to the stove, the better to baste it on the other side, and turning a look of scorn upon this unenlightened cub who was apparently ignorant of the facts of life. "Strong you say? Be the whistlin' jasus I'm tellin' yus he was strong."

A woman of forty with hair the colour of a rusty nail spoke up and praised Murphy's devotion to the Church, Mackenzie King, Sir Wilfrid Laurier, the Pope, the Knights of Columbus and perpetual virginity for the unmarried.

"I long thought that Frank was nugatory," my uncle said piously, looking innocently into his drink.

"Oh that he was, that he was," echoed Gimpy-Leg. "And clever, besides."

"Really nugatory," chimed in the rusty-haired woman. "That was the very word I was gonna say meself. That was Frank all over."

I made myself a promise to look that word up the minute I got home. I saw Elaine shoot a quick glance at Mick, then hastily return to the remains of a salmon sandwich.

Adeline, who had been watching out through a window, went into a flurry as headlights swept the blackness, lighting briefly the yard and the several autos and horse-rigs parked beneath a line of cold spruce trees.

"It's himself," she cried. "Father Devlin has come. John – go out and park the Father's car for him; Brian! where are you, Brian? Brian, be at the door to hand in the priest. Oh Eileen, Eileen darlin'," going to the parlour door and crying in, "it's Father Devlin's come."

As the priest was tenderly ushered in, the people in the kitchen rose and bowed their heads like so many sheep waiting for the butcher. "Good evening, Father" – the murmur running around the room.

He was a man of about forty; fleshy, with a red neck settled well into his clerical collar and the faint beginnings of jowls sprouting below his ears. There was a sleek look to the man – a shine; it was the iridescence of a grackle. In fact, he had the important, half-arrogant strut of a blackbird.

Father Devlin looked keenly from face to face; his eyebrows raised a flutter when he saw Mick who hadn't bent his neck along with the others. The priest nodded shortly, then followed Adeline to the parlour where the keeners again raised their voices, baying their sorrows, real or otherwise, for the benefit of the county at large.

When Adeline returned, Mick said we'd have to be going.

"You're staying for the Rosary, Mike," she protested. Mick shook his head.

"Not tonight, Ad. Seems I neglected to bring my prayer-beads. I've paid my regards to Eileen. . . ."

"You'll be at the funeral Mass?"

"I think it unlikely. If there is anything else we can do. . . ."

The dead man's sister stood uncertainly between us and the door.

"Thanks, Mike – I am glad you came. And I suppose she is, too," ducking her head toward the parlour.

We filed out. The cold, autumn air was bracing after the sterility of that house. I filled my lungs and looked with appreciation at the big, cold stars blinking through the ragged boughs of the spruces.

We all sat in the front seat, Mick driving, on the way home. I liked the way the dash light reflected from Elaine's silk-clad knees. The warmth of her thighs against mine set me trembling. I wondered if Mick felt the same warmth and I thought, jealously, that if he was he had no business doing so.

"You know, Ad used to have quite a crush on me, years ago," he chuckled. "You wouldn't think so, but she's close to my age. Ad was the oldest of the family. Perhaps I should have been flattered; Ad had a penchant for girls – I presume there was a mix-up of hormones somewhere – and there were some ugly stories. She never married, of course; she ran that millinery shop in Lindsay for any number of years. Why is it," turning to Elaine, "that spinster ladies tend to millinery shops?"

"I sensed there is little love lost between you and Father Devlin," Elaine said.

"The Catholic Church has little toleration for a free thinker from its own ranks," Mick answered dryly.

"Do you not believe in God?"

"How do we define 'God'?"

"The God of all those stars." Elaine leaned forward and looked up at the sky through the windshield.

"And that's where He stays," Mick laughed. "He seems little concerned with Earth."

"Buried deeply within the heart of every cynic there is a romantic," Elaine said softly.

"Now that's a very poetic turn of phrase. I rather like it. You will admit, however, that at my age it's wiser to be a cynic than a romantic."

"I'll admit no such thing."

"Then allow me to provide an example. Would it not be better for me to be cynical about . . . let's say you, for instance, than to cherish a romantical notion?"

Elaine studied this over for a moment.

"Does it have to be either-or?"

"Unfortunately – yes."

"Are you asking me something, Mr. Mulcahy?"

"I presume Danny has already done the asking." He let his saturnine smile play about his lips.

"What the hell are you two on about?" All this high-flown give and get-back was too much for me; it made me uncomfortable. I felt Elaine was talking as woman-soft to Mick, as earlier in the day she had to me, and I didn't cotton to it.

The teacher took my hand and stroked it gently between hers.

"I'm beginning to wonder," she murmured.

"What light doth in yonder window shine? . . . Garrity's, without doubt. I hope they haven't locked you out again." Mick swung expertly into the lane and stopped before the front door.

We said our good-nights and Elaine was gone, leaving the faintest trace of fragrance behind her. I studied on it for a time and then decided it reminded me of violets.

"A full-bodied woman, that," Mick said matter-of-factly after we got under way.

"You know, there's times I don't like you very much."

Mick dug a pint flask out of the side pocket of the car, grasped the top between his strong teeth and twisted it off. He swallowed a good third of the bottle, never once taking his eyes from the road ahead.

"Fuck you and what you don't like," he said shortly.

Rage, jealousy and that old fear of him made my voice tremble.

"You're going to come over that bully-boy routine of yours once too often." The implied threat might have had more standing if I could have kept my voice from shaking.

"I could hold you up in the air with one hand until you starved to death," Mick gibed.

We didn't speak again for nearly a week.

TWELVE

The wind, raw and edgy now, kept pretty well to the north. It chased the Canada geese down from the Arctic and the James Bay; all day they peeled across the sky in solemn strings, their heart-breaking cries trailing behind them. The trees that were going to lose their leaves lost them – all save the white oaks where the foliage had turned from russet to a purplish-brown, rustling and clacking with every gust. In the grazing lands, frost turned the water holes black; every morning saw a rim of lace-work ice where only a few months before mother ducks sailed at the head of a convoy of ducklings.

Mick and I hauled hay, from where it had been stacked in the summer, from the middle of October, getting up at the dusk of dawn, shivering our way to the barn in cold drizzle and spiteful sleet alike to harness the team. Fenris always went with us, following the rack-wagon soberly, watchfully, seeming not to be interested in chasing rabbits or getting into the mix-ups and frazzles you can rightfully expect the average mutt to tie in with.

That was the first time I had gone back to the Longford Rocks since Holly died. The Black was running fast and sullen under a lead-grey sky, swollen with the fall rains and cutting meanly at its banks with stray logs and cordwood chunks carried along on the current. I felt the cold hand of the rain on my face and I thought of that same rain falling on a lonely grave in the lee of Bethel church, and for all of what I now thought of Elaine Warren and the promise of something in the future for us, the moisture running down my cheeks wasn't all November rain.

Mick, too, was in a sombre humour, as if the grey fleeting scud represented the gloom of his own thoughts. He had been drinking heavily, even for him, playing his banjo seldom and singing not at all.

He forked hay from the top of the stack down to the rack bed where I built the load, forkful by forkful until it bulged up and over the rack stakes. When we had loaded, we stood in the shelter of the stack and looked at the river creweling its black way to Lake Couchiching.

"John died in the damned thing." Mick spat out his cigarette butt. "It will be forty-four years this spring coming. Your father was about knee high to a rat's ass and Patsy was a babe in arms."

I knew my grandfather had drowned in the Black, but the circumstances I did not know. I had been meaning to inquire from Ed Rilance. Now I asked Mick.

"I thought you knew; seems as if Con didn't talk much about his family. Can't say as I blame him. John was driving the river – running a log drive after the winter's cut. He slipped between two logs, the current caught them and ground them and John together. They pulled his body out somewhere near where the Dallan girl was found."

We awoke one morning to find snow reaching all over as

145

far as eye could see or mind wander. As I ran off a batch of smoking hot pancakes, I was reminded that it was now December and halfway through at that. I also remembered that tonight was the night of the Christmas concert at the 10th Concession school house. My uncle and I had both, yielding to Elaine's entreaties, promised to be on hand.

Since the unpleasantness Mick and I had on the night of Frank Murphy's wake, Elaine was a touchy subject around which both of us footed as lightly as possible. Despite his advantages of education, polish and melodious blarney, I felt that my uncle somehow resented the relationship between the school teacher and myself. While he may have had the strength and looks of a man twenty years younger, Mick was a long way the other side of being youthful and no one realized that better than he did. How much Elaine appealed to him as a woman and how much his vanity was involved, I wasn't sure; we hadn't discussed her since the argument nor had she paid us another visit, although I continued to meet with her on weekends until the weather got too cold for walking around reciting poetry.

The snow continued to fall all through the day, driving hard and fast until every clump of cinquefoil and shrub of hawthorn was mounded to blend in with the white landscape. Mick concluded that winter had arrived with intentions of staying and that the Plymouth would have to sleep away the next few months in the garage. We dug out an ancient cutter that Mick said hadn't been used since Kerwin's time, and set about refurbishing it for the journey to the school house.

Old that sleigh certainly was and at one time it may have been elegant; the runners curled up proudly in front, reversing on themselves like the horns of a mountain goat. Some traces of vermilion enamel clung to the body, and gilt piping was scrolled around the edges. The upholstery on the seat and back rest was a faded crimson and mice had made nests inside. We made the best of what we had – adding a new whipple-tree and running a few screw nails where it appeared they would do the most good.

When we were ready to leave, we threw the single harness on Gertie, backed her between the shalves of the cutter and hooked the traces. Mick located an old set of chime bells in the attic which fitted over the back band of the harness; they made a distinct, if rusty, jingle that was seasonal if nothing else.

The snow had stopped falling and a curt, whiplash wind chased the clouds until the stars came out high and cold and far away. The frost tightened the snow so that the runners squeaked. Mick was looking sporty in a big old buffalo coat and a fur cap and gauntlets.

"This is a genuine buffalo skin taken in death from a genuine buffalo in Montana. There are even genuine warble-fly holes in the thing to prove it."

"Well, I'm impressed," I said, grinning. "But will it keep you warm?"

"When was the last time you heard of a buffalo freezing to death?" asked Mick amiably.

We cut diagonally across the ranch, heading southwest to line up with the school house. I had some almighty reservation about Christmas concerts; I didn't shine much to school kids to begin with; to be jammed into a cracker box of a school house with twenty or so of them for three or four hours was not my idea of a night's frolic.

"Why are you going to this shindy, anyhow?" I asked Mick.

"Partly because I'm on the school board; partly because Miss Warren spent last Saturday in Lindsay shopping for a suitable frock for the occasion and I am eager to see how she appears in it. See that star there – the bright one to your left? That is Betelgeuse. I understand it's a good deal bigger than our sun."

"And right now we're getting just about as much heat from it. I didn't know Elaine went to Lindsay just for a dress." I felt powerfully aggrieved that I hadn't been told and that Mick had. I sensed a betrayal. The dogs of jealousy began snapping at my heels.

"I don't suppose there's any reason why she should send you a special delivery informing you of the fact," said Mick, affably. "I heard all about it from Ed Rilance who had it straight from Mrs. Garrity. You see the way news gets around here in Brulé, Danny.

147

"It seems there is a coolness – a studied difference of opinion between Doris Rilance and Miss Warren. Now why do you suppose that would be?"

"I haven't got the slightest god damned notion." I shrugged and pretended to be studying up on Betelgeuse.

"I think it's time for a drink." Mick reached into the folds of the lap robe and brought forth a bottle. The pronged moon, as cold and metallic as the sky it sailed in, bounced feeble glints off the glass.

Mick saluted the moon with the bottle. "First – a toast:

Here's to mugs, cups and glasses,
Here's to the man who has two lasses;
He loves the one and fucks the other –
That's what I call a two-faced bugger.

The school house windows blazed with gas light. A few automobiles and several sleighs and cutters were ranged around the yard, the latter with horses under heavy blankets, their breath steamy and glittering in the frosted moonlight.

Inside, a festive air, unusual for Brulé, flourished beneath the hissing gas lamps hanging from hooks in the ceiling. The windows were decked out in paper cut-outs reflecting the kids' idea of what holly wreaths looked like, and Elaine had artistically drawn Nativity scenes and other Christmasy things with coloured chalk on the blackboards. Red and green crepe-paper streamers, twisted round, ran from corner to corner with a big paper bell in red dangling from the point where they met in the centre. Across the front of the room where the teacher's desk normally stood was a plank stage across which was drawn a set of old green curtains strung on sagging wires. Footsteps pattered mysteriously behind these curtains which occasionally bumped and swayed like a bagful of small pigs. A huge spruce tree hung 'round within an inch of its life with tinsel, glass birds and balls, strings of gold and silver ropes, and weighted with packages, stood fair beneath the ceiling in a corner next to the stage.

There must have been close to a hundred mixed gentry crammed inside the school: low Irish life from Slab Town;

Indians of full blood and fractions thereof from Dog Town; lace-curtain Irish from the south end of the township, and an Anglo-Saxon element leaning heavily toward Fundamentalism and the benefits of Total Immersion from the purlieus of Bethel church and the metropolis of Northmore.

Northmore had a school of sorts complete with a teacher of sorts – a small, brown gnome of a woman by the name of Harriet Sprule who had attended a teachers' college for nearly three months and had never gotten over the shock of finding out that her instructors didn't take their biology from Genesis. Miss Sprule was one of those hapless females doomed to perpetual spinsterhood from the minute they're hauled forth, damp and dripping, from the recesses of the womb. Such women appear to have been born at the age of forty-seven; one doesn't imagine them ever playing with dolls, wearing a party dress or playing An-Inch-Or-Two-Or-Three-Above-Your-Pretty-Knee under the lap robe on the way home from the box social. Miss Sprule, knowing very little and suspecting a great deal, was in a sweat to disseminate her ignorance among the young; she reigned five days a week at Northmore school and on Sundays she dealt out Psalms and Proverbs with the hand of a tyrant in the basement of Bethel Church, her musty Bible propped against the hot air pipe of the wood furnace. She warned her little charges, in a doom-wracked voice, that God was a jealous God girt 'round with thunder and lightnings and armed to the teeth with a fiery sword which was going to help Him powerfully when the Great Day came to judge the living, the dead, and those that hung out in Slab Town.

Although I didn't know it at the time, Elaine had the idea of joining the Brulé and Northmore schools for the purpose of putting on a grand concert, combining the immense talent of both these institutions of the higher learning. Knowing that her city ways would be suspicioned, she enlisted Uncle Mick, who could charm a bird out of a bush or Miss Sprule out of her knee-length cotton drawers if he took the notion, to spring the suggestion to the educational authorities of Northmore; Elaine would work on the powers in Brulé. Mick by-passed the Sprule person and took the case to the Reverend Artemus Peckinpaugh, minister in residence of Bethel Church and

149

shepherd to the lambs, rams and ewes of Somerset Township and the overflow from Longford. Peckinpaugh, Peckinpaugh's severe wife, and the Peckinpaugh progeny to the number of six, lived in a bare, bleak manse on the edge of Northmore.

Northmore was renowned for having more streets than it did houses or commercial establishments combined. In earlier times, two men with leather folders and a new buggy with red wheels, rented from the livery in Riverdale, had laid out a town site with streets, avenues, boulevards, plats, lots, parks and a place for a city hall with a running fountain and a horse trough. A few houses were built and a few people moved in; then the men melted away on the afternoon train; the streets were never filled with houses and a family named Bilson pastured their milk cow where the park was supposed to be. There remained one general store, one garage and gas pump, a few unpainted clapboard houses and a town dump that was visited by bears that came down from Longford and swam the Black every night for the fun of turning over empty bean cans.

When Mick rapped on the door it was opened by Mrs. Peckinpaugh, a woman as upright as a pine knot and nearly as curvaceous. He doffed his hat, flashed his teeth, professed admiration for her youthfulness which, Mick claimed, always made him feel his advancing years, and inquired for her husband. Peckinpaugh was in his study laying out next Sunday's sermon of wrath. He was a tall beanpole of a man, with an Adam's-apple that bobbed up and down like a yo-yo in a milk bottle. He had a perpetual croupy hack that played rough with his pulpit delivery, and a watery turn of eye from witnessing the onslaught of sin around him, plus a wistful look from his inability to see more.

"Well, well, Brother Mulcahy!" He got up and thrust out a clammy hand which Mick thoughtfully ground to the knuckles in his own massive paw. "We don't often see you up our way." The preacher turned his head and coughed into a blue bandana.

"You must excuse my asthma – it's this damp of winter – always gets to my lungs. . . ."

Mick was a tower of sympathy.

"I know," he nodded. "I am similarly afflicted. I believe it's a judgement against us for the follies and excesses of wanton youth. But my physician, who studied in Vienna under the great Seidlitz, prescribes for me a nostrum he refines himself: Dr. Fleer's Effluvia of Rheum. Perhaps you've tried it?"

Peckinpaugh shook his head.

"Then allow me." Mick produced an innocent medicine bottle which he had loaded with white rum.

"*Hmmmm* – do you think it might work? Miriam . . . dear . . . will you bring a teaspoon?"

"Bring a water glass, Miriam," suggested Mick.

After draining the second glass the preacher allowed as how he felt a gentle warmth stealing through him. Halfway through the third he wanted to know the name and address of the doctor who manufactured this Affluent of Ruin. By the time Mick left, Peckinpaugh had embraced him, called him a Fellow in Christ, and thoroughly agreed that the two schools should join hands in putting on a concert in celebration of the Birth of the Lamb. He would get hold of Miss Sprule that very afternoon and see to it that she co-operated in every way. Mrs. Peckinpaugh showed Mick out while her husband sang "Jehovah, Now Thy Kingdom Rule" with some energy.

The collaboration was not without a certain touchiness: when the Brulé school was being decorated, a select committee composed of Mrs. Peckinpaugh, Mrs. Bilson and Mrs. Homer Clow called and looked about critically. The gilt angel Elaine had fashioned from a Kewpie doll, tissue paper, and the wings from a stuffed screech owl, and fastened to the top candle of the Christmas tree was, declared Mrs. Peckinpaugh, "too 'Catholic' looking." Mrs. Clow muttered something about "bowing down to graven images." The angel was demoted and replaced by a large and, presumably, Protestant star.

The front row of seats closest to the stage was occupied by fry of an age too young for school and too old to be toted. Directly behind them were mothers with babes at the carry, mothers with babes at the slope, and mothers-soon-to-be. Then came single women and girls with and without hopes. Included in this batch, I noticed, was Doris Rilance, her brown eyes sparkling with an eagerness to get critical. Then were seated the married men, the respectable men, the aged and infirm. Ranged standing against the rear wall were the riff and raff and a drunk who had wandered in out of the frost to get warm. There was a great commingling of unnatural odours: cheap face powder, barnyard smells, wet wool socks and the crisp fragrance of fir boughs taped to the walls above the blackboards.

When the place had filled to the point where you couldn't have squeezed a Barnum midget inside without using a tire iron, the curtains pulled creakily back to show the stage and the student body lined up thereon in a semi-circle. Elaine, looking sexy and beautiful in a yellow knitted sweater and a pleated skirt of the same colour, stood in front and in a lovely, clear voice that shook only a little said how delighted she was to see such a large turn-out and that she hoped we would enjoy the presentation to follow. She then turned the show over to the preacher who was master of ceremonies.

The Reverend Peckinpaugh arose, fixed his gaze on the ceiling and informed God that we were all there. He called for a blessing on the school, the pupils, the faculty and the trustees. I think he would have asked a blessing on the pigeons that had a home up in the belfry if he'd known they were there. The blessings and orisons out of the road, Peckinpaugh scanned the bill of fare and declared that little Melvin Hodge was going to deliver a recital.

Melvin was a snotty-nosed little wart with a dreadful lisp brought about by his having a hare-lip; for my money he had a hare-brain to match. He trotted out, got all red in the face and sputtered the following gem:

> We wis' oo all a vewy mewy Ch'wis'mass –
> We hope – we – *ahhh, awwww, we ahhhhh. . . .*
> We *oooopps – awwwww. . . .*

Having got thus far and no farther, Melvin collapsed into tears and fled to the wings amid thunderous applause, while his mother got all red-faced and proud and looked around to see if the audience realized it was her Melvin who had so nobly acquitted himself.

There were carols and dialogues and recitations. One play had Mother sitting forlornly by the fire, gazing at a row of empty stockings pinned to a cardboard fireplace and saying to Father: "Oh dear, here it is Christmas Eve and we are so poor there is nothing to put in the children's stockings!" The day is saved when a troop of squirrels passing by the window hear the lament and rush about gathering acorns and what-have-you and chunking them in the stockings. Tod Ryan as a squirrel, the tail-piece from his mother's fox fur coat sticking out of the seat of his pants, had to be seen to be believed.

Among Miss Sprule's talents was a pretension to playing the piano; the piano was much out of tune and so was the player, but after the dialogues had ended, Miss Sprule struck up a lively air and out bounced a couple of fifteen-year-old heifers in short skirts and proceeded to perform a tandem step-dance that was a cross between the Can-Can and the Slab Town Stomp. It was not all that bad; the girls had real good legs and they showed them clear up to the little black tights that, as I learned later, Elaine had manufactured with the use of the Garrity treadle sewing machine. A sort of hush enveloped the assemblage while Miss Sprule, eyes averted, thumped dazedly at the keyboard as if this was none of her doings and that she was merely co-operating as ordered. Then, August Clow, who hadn't seen so much bare thigh since the day he was married and maybe not then, let out a piercing whistle – a whistle cut off in mid-blast by a look from his wife which promised plenty in the way of a lecture when she got him home. The riff and the rakes standing at the back began to whistle and clap and pretty soon the rest of the men-folk took it up until the gas lamps were set swinging.

From the Fundamentalist section, particularly the distaff side, there were a lot of "Well, I never"s and "Did you ever see the like"s. Doris Rilance's smirk of satisfaction could be heard out loud.

The preacher, who sat through the step-dance without being quite sure whether to applaud or sink to his knees and pray for deliverance, clambered to his feet and waved a yellow sheet of paper that he swore was a telegram just delivered from the

North Pole. Sandy Claws, he said, was on his way and would be here any minute. A set of bells began jangling outside the window.

"There!" said the preacher triumphantly. "There Santy is – right on time."

Tod Ryan piped up that it might well be Santy, but that sure was Semper Garrity's sleigh bells.

It was not only Garrity's bells, it was Semper himself trigged out in a red suit and a set of whiskers. At least he didn't require any pillows stuffed down the front of his pants; Semper had the natural qualifications for the job in that respect.

As Santa was bawling out the names of the kids getting presents, Mick asked me what I thought Father Christmas had fetched along for the teacher. I had a sudden numbness in the hollow of my stomach.

"I never thought of getting her a present."

"You," said my uncle, "are an oaf and a dullard."

For once I didn't argue.

I couldn't take any more of the jollity and the ho ho ho. I got my coat and slipped outside and took the blanket off the mare. Mick joined me.

"It's a fine night for a walk and I wish to contemplate the stars. You knew, of course, that Miss Warren expects you to drive her home after the merry ball."

"I didn't get her anything," I said miserably.

"Well, don't tell her that – you'll make liars out of both of us. One in the family is sufficient." Mick secured his bottle from under the cutter seat, checked it to see if it was frozen, and stalked away beneath the moon.

I waited around until most of the people had filed out and driven away. Then I went in the rear door and found Elaine sprawled exhausted in a chair, a huge, expensively-wrapped gift box in her arms.

"Oh Danny!" she cried. "I thought you'd forgotten all about me. I haven't even opened your lovely present yet. Do you know you were the only one in the entire township that remembered me?"

I opened and closed my mouth several times like a beached flounder.

154

She tugged at the wrappings. "I just have to look. I'm so thrilled."

When she got the package opened, she slowly removed a sky-blue négligé, a silk slip and a very brief pair of panties of the same colour and satiny material.

"Oh Dan-ee!" she squealed.

She set the things down and threw her arms around me and kissed me full on the mouth and kept on kissing me as if Miss Sprule, who had ducked behind the curtains to where we were, wasn't watching and taking notes.

"But I've never had anything so sexy and beautiful," Elaine exulted, holding the lingerie up for Miss Sprule to admire.

"Must of went clear to Lindsay for that outfit." Miss Sprule was not at all approving. "Looks like something a man would buy – or a boy."

That "boy" remark triggered my temper. I was set to say something cruel and appropriate, but Elaine was ahead of me.

"Only if he was in love," she said sweetly.

I helped turn out the gas lights, lock up the school, and hand the Sprule woman into Peckinpaugh's ancient Ford coach. Mrs. Peckinpaugh had a thing or three on her mind about the concert and she wasn't about to slip anchor until she'd relieved herself on the matter.

"I don't know, young woman, where you came up with that notion of dancing. *Dancing* – mind you! As if there wasn't enough vulgarity these days. . . ."

I was real glad of a chance to take the cutting edge of my temper out on somebody.

"Well, you ought to know all about vulgarity. Northmore is the heart and home of that commodity and you're as good a representative of that hole as you'd locate in a day's marching."

The reverend tried to inflate himself within his layers of overcoats.

"Tut! I say – tut, my boy. Some respect to your elders – need I say your betters."

"You needn't, but if you do I'll haul you out of that broken down jumble of nuts and bolts and kick you so god damned hard you'll be wearing the cheeks of your bony arse for earrings."

I grabbed Elaine by the elbow and hustled her over to the cutter, settled her against the cushions and tucked the lap robe about her, feeling the firmness of her hips as I did so. I hit the mare a swat with the lines and we skittered down the road, the snow flying from the sharp-shod hooves of the horse to pelt against the dashboard.

When we reached a long stretch of road that passed through a swamp and was fringed on either side by a rank taggle of alders, I stopped the rig and, with hands that were still trembling with anger, rolled a cigarette. I wasn't very good at it and the paper tore, letting the tobacco spill out over the lap robe.

Elaine looked at me and I looked at her. The bare alder branches framed against the moonlight threw a pattern of crisses and crosses about her face. She was in my arms then, nestled against me under the robe and my hands, still trembling, were reaching under her skirt.

And when it was over and finished she didn't whimper or cry or babble about how we shouldn't have done it. She sat there quietly, her skirt still hiked up and the moonlight winking on the metal fasteners of her garter-straps. There was a kind of sadness in her eyes and a kind of happiness, with one struggling against the other and her not at all sure which would win out.

"I wasn't a virgin," she whispered.

"No," I said, "you weren't."

"For you I should have been, Danny."

"What does it matter?" I said fiercely.

"I thought it was terribly important to men."

"I'm only a boy – remember." I was still bitter.

"Oh, but you're very much a man – so very much a man. And Danny – that's the awful thing. You should have a youth and a boyhood and not be plunged into the frenetic adult world without experiencing the beauty of being young.

"Besides," she teased, "only a very mature man would know exactly what to buy a girl at Christmas."

"Right as Jesus."

"Don't be cross. I love your gift. Danny – I love you. Danny, Danny! I love you."

THIRTEEN

The reigning school board of the 10th Concession, Brulé, was composed of a chairman (Semper Garrity) and four trustees. Besides Uncle Mick, John Sullivan, Fairleigh Downs and Jack Connolly – all small graziers – made up the roster of the board.

Between Christmas and the New Year, when Elaine was away for the school holiday, the board had a conclave in the school house. By a solemn vote of four to one the teacher was condemned for sponsoring and abetting the production of a lewd performance – to wit, a dancing act calculated to affect the moral character of dancers and viewers alike. By a similar vote it was decreed that the remainder of her contract be bought up, and that Elaine be denounced to the Provincial Department of Education as immoral, unfit and indecent. A registered letter was

157

despatched, informing Miss Warren of the same, to her home.

Mick alone cast the nay vote. Apparently he cast it Mulcahy fashion: Semper Garrity had his nose broken; John Sullivan was thrown down the front steps; Jack Connolly could see from neither eye for two weeks. Fairleigh Downs was unscathed, having taken flight across fields knee-deep in snow, forgetting in his haste his horse and cutter.

The following day, while Mick soaked his swollen right hand in brine water, he provided me with his opinion of the democratic process, the cast-iron composition of all skulls belonging to school boards, and a few general comments on sad-assed, puritanical sons-of-bitches individually and collectively.

"Politics finds an odd assortment under the blankets," he raved. "It was that pinch-faced Peckinpaugh bitch that started the ball rolling. She went to Devlin – that long-nosed arbiter of the public good – and he twisted the weak Dogan arms of Garrity, Connolly and that jack-ass, Sullivan. Downs isn't Catholic, but he's too cowardly to buck the current. I wish I'd got my hands around his scrawny throat. . . ."

I answered a banging on the kitchen door. Brad-Awl Callum was standing in the blizzard. He brushed past me, stamping his boots on the floor to rid them of the snow they had accumulated between the Riverdale road and the house.

"I hae here," he rasped, pulling a paper out of his mackinaw, "a warrant for your arrest on the complaint of sundry members of yon school board who upon oath before the Justice of the Peace did swear that upon the. . . ."

Mick took a bottle out of the cupboard, sat down at the table and poured himself a drink.

"Brad-Awl," he said pleasantly, "I admire your sense of duty. I do dislike your methods. Ever since you and I tangled many years ago I've promised myself the pleasure of killing you. Today may be the time."

"Are ye resistin' an officer on his lawful course, Mulcahy?"

"No. I'm going to shoot a son of a whore's bastard that has lived far too long for his own good and that of everyone else. Danny, get my rifle."

I looked quickly at Mick. I realized he was drunk – mean, ornery drunk.

"You don't want your rifle."

Mick drained and refilled his glass. "Don't tell me what I want or don't want. Brad-Awl – you make another move toward that rusty pea-shooter of yours and I'll cave your skull with this bottle. . . ."

The constable unbuckled his worn old Sam Browne, slipped out of his mackinaw and carefully hung belt and holster on the back of a chair.

"I'll no fight ye wi' guns, Mulcahy. Ootside wi' ye – we'll hae to settle scores there."

Mick nodded. For all his apparent calmness there was a wild, fearsome glare in his eyes. I felt cold inside – cold and frightened like the day the Mountie came to the school house in Alberta.

For the second time in a score of years Brad-Awl and my uncle fought. They fought out in the yard, tramping the snow heavily, panting, swinging, stopping to rest – then slashing cruelly at each other again. Blood dripped down Mick's face, dripped down his torn shirt to be lost in the whirling snow storm that raged around both men so thickly that at times they were nearly blotted from sight where I stood on the verandah. Brad-Awl's face looked as if a horse had stepped on it; a ragged gash had opened the side of his mouth.

Mick leaped and swung his injured right hand; he struck the policeman high on the head, wincing. Brad-Awl landed his enormous fist like a club to the side of Mick's jaw; he dropped flat on his face, rolled over, shook his head and edged dazedly to one knee. Brad-Awl staggered forward and shot his boot out toward Mick's face; my uncle caught the foot in both hands, rose to his feet and twisted. There was a crack like a deep frost in the sapwood of a spruce and Brad-Awl screamed, then fell back in the blinding snow, his leg twisted at an odd angle.

With awful deliberation Mick leaned over and fastened his powerful hands about the throat of the fallen man.

"Ye've won, Mulcahy. Finish it and be domned to ye," Brad-Awl's eyes bulged with pain, but without fear.

"Stand clear, Uncle Mick," I said. I aimed his .30.30 and levered a cartridge into the breech.

He turned his head and peered at me through the blizzard. He wiped the blood that was seeping into his eyes and shook his head.

"You wouldn't shoot!"

"I'll shoot you right in the leg. I happen to like you, god damn it to hell, and I'd shoot you before I'd let them hang you for killing that ignorant Scotch bastard."

Slowly, he got up. He looked down at Brad-Awl, then back at me.

"I believe you would."

He walked unsteadily into the house; his face, beneath the blood, was old and grey and drawn. The door closed behind him.

I took Brad-Awl to Horncastle in the cutter, and I had a hard job of it, getting him loaded into the sleigh with his leg bent sideways like a broken match-stick. He never said a word all the way and he didn't utter a single groan. I didn't like him but he had grit – I'll give him that.

I ran in the store and got Ed Rilance, and between the two of us we got Brad-Awl into Rilance's car and the storekeeper took him to Riverdale, although we had to put chains on the car wheels so that he could navigate the storm.

My uncle went to court in Lindsay after New Year's and was fined twenty dollars for common assault. Brad-Awl explained to his county superiors that he slipped and fell while delivering the warrant, and Ed Rilance had a brand new story to tell around the Quebec heater in his store on long winter evenings.

Sometime in January of 1932, Elaine wrote me a letter to say that she had a teaching position away out in the western part of the province near a place called Petrolia. She said the Brulé school board must have changed their minds about black-listing her with the Department of Education – that instead she was given an excellent recommendation.

Actually, there wasn't very much in the letter, and I was disappointed, although I was glad she had a new school. I thought after what had happened and what she'd said on the way home from the Christmas concert she would have stuck in a lot more affection instead of what she did.

I sat at the table with a lined tablet and Mick's big orange Waterman's fountain pen and set about writing my first letter to Elaine. I tried to imitate my uncle's flowing copper-plate script, but it all came out like turkey tracks anyway, so I gave up trying to make waves and curlicues and forged ahead with my own brand of penmanship, which was hardly orderly, but could always be read in a good light.

Dear Elaine –

Your letter came ok and I was glad to hear from you and to know you are back teaching again. I think my uncle talked to the Brulé school board. He is in the kitchen here with me, playing his banjo and singing pretty dirty songs. He isn't so strong on manners when there is no woman around.

Things is just about the same here – I mean – are just about the same. My grammar keeps slipping since you left. I guess I need you to teach me lots yet. We just feed the cattle in the open lot and keep the fires burning. I seen – saw – old man Garrity yesterday. His nose is still flat.

I was talking to Doris Rilance. I think I will take her to a talking picture in Lindsay if they get the road ploughed out. There is lots of snow. I never seen a talking picture yet. Mick says its bad enough having to see Fatty Arbuckle without having to hear him as well. I hope Doris likes the show.

I have been reading that guy Browning. I liked the one about April in England. I wish April was here now. I guess I wish a lot of things.

I don't suppose you will want to come back this way, ever. I will miss you. I wish you were going to the show with me instead of Doris Rilance. Every time I hear the train whistles I think of you.

I guess I might leave here come springtime. There isn't too much left here for me, I don't guess. I think I might go and get a job on a tramp freighter and see places and different things.

I hope you think of me once in a while.

All my love
Danny.

161

Mick had his sock feet up on the warm reservoir of the range; he felt out an air on the banjo.

> I once loved a lass and I loved her so well
> I hated all others who spoke of her ill;
> And now she has paid me right well for my love –
> She's gone to be wed to another.

"My hand hasn't been right since the ruckus," he complained. "The fingers become numb. Did you notice I went astray on a couple of notes?"

I put on my fur-lined parka and got my snowshoes from the back porch. For the first time since I came to Brulé to live, old Fenris got up from his bed of gunny-sacks in back of the stove and followed me. I must have tramped miles, with the wind straight out of the bitter black north bringing on its crest the muted wail of steam locomotives heading north along the main line.

I remember reaching the Culm, frozen hard now, all save a strip in the middle where the current kept the river free of ice. That strip looked black and fearsome, throwing back the hard, silver reflection of the stars. Somewhere across the river in Longford a timber wolf howled; another answered from farther away; and another. Fenris sat close against my legs, shivering. He threw back his head and forced out a low, rising moan that seemed to hang in the air for a moment before the wind caught it and travelled it across the drifting snow and lost it somewhere far to the south.

I threw back the hood of my parka and leaned my forehead against the bole of a pine tree. The wind cut through the dry, frozen needles, singing a cruel air, singing of winter and ice and frozen dreams. I thought I was going to cry. I was remembering another day and another pine tree and Elaine and I sitting on the rust-brown needles that had fallen in a carpet. I was remembering how the wind sang a different tune that day – soft and sweet and as gentle as a harp crooning an Irish air. I remembered how her legs had looked beneath her shorts and how they looked in the cutter on the way to Garrity's from the school house.

162

I looked at the open place on the river for a long time. I thought of how easy it would be to just walk out and drop into the black, yawning current and let it carry me away and down like the Black River had carried my grandfather and Holly Dallan. And I wondered if I did that would Uncle Mick write to Elaine and tell her and would she grieve just a little.

I snowshoed out a couple of yards onto the ice, attracted by the eager call of the river. The swift waters fascinated me, drew me on. "Come," sang the river. "Come and join me. My waters are cold but you will not feel the cold. My stream is fast but you will not know how fast. Come," the river crooned. "Come and join me."

Fenris whined and followed me reluctantly; his dull claws skidded on the ice. He whined again and gripped my trouser leg in his teeth. I turned and made my way back to shore. Mick was standing under the pine, rolling a smoke.

"I was just going to have a social chat with George Heeney," he said, digging around in his side pocket for his lighter. "I thought I could cross the river about here, but I can see it's still open in places."

On the way home Mick pointed out a star he said was Aldebaran.

A mean blizzard, which February often brings to this part of the country, was howling down clear from Gravenhurst. The shutters banged and rattled for all of the fixing I'd done on them, and the wind was one steady moan about the eaves.

George Heeney staggered through the snow and gale late in the afternoon and poured himself a mug of coffee from the blue granite pot on the back of the stove.

"Say that's a mighty mean day out." He spat carefully into the wood-box. "I just come from the store. The mail just got in. Hank Brewster had the team on the mail sleigh today; said the goin' was pretty heavy between here and Riverdale."

The old man hitched out of his heavy coat and threw the Toronto paper on the table.

"Here's your *Star*, Mick. Oh yeah – I got a letter fer the younker, here. Where did I put the gol' damn thing. Here it

163

is. Pew – it stinks. Musta been dipped in a barr'l o' yo dee calumny."

"Give me that letter! If there's any stink it's from being next to your dirty underwear." I grabbed the envelope and took it into the library to read it in privacy. It was from Elaine all right, but there was no smell of perfume. That was one of old Heeney's crude barges at being humorous.

Dearest Danny,

Oh Danny, how sorry I am that you miss me and are so lonely. But darling I miss you too – I can't tell you how much. I was so afraid that – well – that we were both too young. Now I am sure everything will be all right between us. You are my man, Danny. I know that. I just hope, darling, that I am your woman. I don't care how long we have to wait. I will wait forever.

Don't you dare take that dreadful Doris person *anywhere*, Danny Mulcahy, or I'll come straight up there and scratch her eyes out.

Danny, write and tell me you love me – and please, please – don't go away on some old ship where I'll never see you again. I have nearly two weeks holiday at Easter. I'll come and spend them with you at Brulé if you want me. Do you want me? I want you. . . .

I love you
Elaine.

I rushed back to the kitchen, waving Elaine's letter. The two men were deep in reminiscences and hardly noticed that I was galloping around the room with my head scraping the ceiling.

"Do you remember the Burkes?" Mick was saying to Heeney.

"Yes, I mind them well. Hiram Burke. Lived over in a hollow alongside Scattergood Crik. Where'd that crik run to? The Culm or the Black? I think it was the Black. Wasn't there three girls? Seems to me one married a Fogarty."

"Yes, there were three girls: Minnie, Johanna and Maude." Mick leaned back and cradled his head in his clasped hands, which was always a sign he was getting set to pull off some long-winded yarn.

"This would be about – oh – around 1881. Anyway, Hiram was as lazy as a pet coon, and they had this back-house. Hiram built it on two logs he'd thrown across the creek; it was handy that way because he never had to clean it out – everything washed down with the creek water. This shanty was about two hundred yards away from the house. Well, on summer days some of us young lads would get up in the hills above the little valley drained by the Scattergood, and with a stopwatch and a pair of field glasses we would clock the girls from the time they left the back door until they reached the out-house. We used to lay bets on which girl made the fastest time.

"Minnie was the fastest as a general rule; she had long legs and a great turn of speed. When the track was fast and the wind right, Minnie was the horse to back.

"Johanna was a good mudder. In deep snow or after a heavy rain, Johanna was odds-on to take the roses. She was low-slung with a hefty pair of shalves on her.

"Maude was the hard one to tout. I've seen Maude turtle along and take two and a half minutes to cover the stretch. Another time when a thunder storm came up, she was out the back door and into the shit-shack in twenty seconds flat.

"Well sir, one morning I walked into Riverdale to Mass – Father Daly was the priest then – and I had this plan up my sleeve. You remember old Mrs. Burke and how fat she was – must have weighed nearly three hundred on the hoof. . . ."

George grunted. "She'd of went that gutted and without her liver and lights."

"No one of us in his right mind would have thought of betting on the old lady. My Jesus to Judas, no! It so happened she had a sweet tooth – loved candy. I went to Krail's confectionery shop after Mass and I bought a half-pound of chocolate drops and slipped a few grains of tartar emetic in every last one of them. The Burkes had been to Mass with their old horse and side-seat cart and I overtook them on the way home as they were ambling up the 10th.

" 'How are you, Mr. Burke, Missis Burke,' I says, being a

polite bastard, even then. 'Would the girls like some candy?'
I knew who was going to eat the candy.

"On in the afternoon, the gang of us: there was Paddy Driscoll
and Liam Duggan and Martin White and a couple of others
. . . we got up on the hill with our stopwatch and our field
glasses and started laying our bets. It was a fine, clear summer's
day, so naturally the big money was all on Minnie – she could
sprint like a gazelle. I think Liam bet Johanna because there
had been a rain the night before and the course was slippery.
I had five dollars I'd borrowed from father – big money in those
days. I put the whole wad on the old woman.

"Well George, you should have heard the laughter. They put
it down to another Mad Mulcahy piece of foolishness and
covered my money.

"First out was Maude. She stopped to pick flowers or stomp
a garter-snake or some other fool thing. Maude was out of the
running. Johanna wasn't having one of her better days, either;
she made it in 1:17. But Minnie gave me a bad turn. Minnie
came flying out and turned in one of her best times, ever.
Twenty-two seconds by the clock.

"Minnie was hardly back in the house when the rear door
flew open and out boiled the old woman in what might best
be described as a fat blur. She was down the path and into
the toilet with a momentum that threatened to take her clean
through and on out into the creek. Martin White was on the
stopwatch and he ran around like a crazy man. 'Fifteen seconds!'
he was yelling. 'Fifteen seconds! An' the ould wan takes the
sweeps, the crown and the derby!' "

"I don't believe a word of that," I said, grinning from ear
lug to postern. "Where's the jug, Uncle Mick, I need a drink."

FOURTEEN

The trial of Toot Finnerty, after several fits and starts and post-ponements, came to pass. It wasn't much of a trick for twelve men and a judge to find the defendant guilty of a reduced charge of manslaughter, although what processes of reasoning they employed to decide that Oliver O'Kane was a man, I can't say. The County Judge sentenced Toot to seven years at hard labour and sent him back to the common gaol in Lindsay until a sheriff's officer could slap him in manacles and haul him off to Kingston to serve his term.

The day after the trial, we were surprised at breakfast by Tanglefoot's appearance at the back door. She had slogged through knee-high snow, soft and granular from a three-day March thaw, all the way from Slab Town. The woman stood on the porch, wet and with her bare red legs shoved into a pair of men's rubber boots some several sizes too much for her. She looked like something that had melted on the roof, dripped to the porch floor and re-frozen.

"Tanglefoot – you're out at an unseemly hour. Taking the spring airs, no doubt. Have you breakfasted? I think there are a couple of fried eggs in the pan. Have some coffee in the meantime."

Mick set out a mug and filled it with java.

"Mister Mulcahy – you heard about Toot?"

"I heard he is bound for seven years at hard labour. The County hasn't succeeded in getting seven minutes of anything approaching hard labour from Toot in thirty-six years. I doubt that the penitentiary system will be more successful."

"Toot was my man," Tanglefoot said defensively.

"He was *one* of your men. The other is dead. One dead and one away; two from two leaves nothing. Are you looking about for replacements? You might consider Danny. He is young but able. Or how about George Heeney? Your housekeeping styles are greatly similar; you would feel right at home after you carried each other across the threshold. Come to think of it, George no longer has a threshold: he was forced to burn it during the last blizzard."

I knew Mick had a long memory and carried a grudge until it wore out from being packed around so long, but I hadn't considered his dislike of Finnerty had extended to Tanglefoot. I thought his baiting was cruel and unneedful. I was beginning to feel sorry for the creature.

"Mr. Mulcahy," she began with a dignity that surprised me and may have surprised Mick, "I want to see Toot before he is sent away to Kingston, and I don't know how to get to Lindsay to the jail to see him. I don't have no money – none at all. No," she lifted her hand when Mick reached for his wallet, "I don't want any money giv' to me. I didn't come to beg nothing. I came to ask you as a good man I know you are to take me to Lindsay to see Toot one more time before he goes."

It wasn't often I had the chance to see my uncle discomfitted. He was now and I purely enjoyed the sight of it. But he had that feline instinct that always landed him right side up and on his feet no matter how far he fell or what dropped him to start with.

"Tanglefoot," he lied, "I'm glad you dropped over. You have saved me a trip. I was about to go to Slab Town this very morning and inquire if you wished to go along to visit Toot. You see, it so happens I have to drive to Lindsay and it crossed my mind you would like to get together with Toot ere he departs."

It was a good try and I applauded inside, but Tanglefoot was having none of it.

"No, Mr. Mulcahy, it's good of you to say all that, but you didn't have no such intentions and you don't need to be kind. I don't want your kindness no more than I want this coffee here," she shoved the mug away from her, untouched. "But if you can take me to Lindsay I'll be in your debt, I will, truly. And you needn't bother about taking me back. I can get back all right."

Mick went over to the window and looked out for a long time without saying anything. A slow burn worked its way up the back of his neck.

"Back to what, Angela?" he said at last. He said it slowly, and it was the first time I had heard anyone use Tanglefoot's rightly given name. In fact it was the first time I'd ever heard it. I thought it was a pretty name and I wondered how come it was tagged onto her in the first place and why nobody, not even its owner, ever used it.

"Back to that house, there," she answered quietly.

"Danny, warm the car engine, will you?" There was a kind of desperation in Mick's look.

Mick and I kicked around Lindsay while we waited for Tanglefoot to come out of the brick gaol with its barred windows and the town sparrows quarrelling and rousting around the steep-pitched roof gables. The snow in town was dirtier than in the country; it was flecked with soot and patches of coal dust and the peculiar brown over-scum an urban place casts over all but the freshest of newly-fallen snow. The day was grey and depressing and both of us felt that depression. We went into the Chinaman's and ordered pie and coffee.

169

"What would you give Tanglefoot for a present, supposing you were God or Clifford Stackpole – which is next thing to it?"

I thought on that a minute.

"Well, I'd go and buy her a nice dress and a warm coat and some decent shoes and stockings."

"Yes, you would. And a week later the dogs and cats and great grey rats would be making nests in all that finery, and Tanglefoot would be back in her rubber boots and sackcloth and ashes.

"No, we will buy Tanglefoot a present: a case of Bright's Catawba. There's nothing she would appreciate more."

I argued that there seemed to be a lot of good in the woman and that under the right circumstances she would turn a new hitch and come out right in the wind-up. Mick shook his head.

"For the Tanglefoots of this world there are never any right circumstances. The process of disintegration started, perhaps, while she was still in the womb. Her mother was a slut and her father may have been any one or a dozen of the bums that hang around in that gift-box of the god-forsaken. You cannot make a silk purse out of a sow's ear, although, oddly enough, you can make a passable sow's ear out of a silk purse."

On the drive back, Tanglefoot got thoroughly into her case of cheap sherry and puked all over the rear seat.

"There's your silken sow's ear," said Mick, wryly.

As the winter wore away and spring showed itself in the form of a very black crow which perched in the top of a Lombardy poplar and sent its long dark call across the hillocks brown and bare beneath the watery sun, Mick complained more and more about his right hand. It had grown very painful and he was unable to use it in any way. He made a couple of trips to Lindsay to have a doctor look at the hand.

"I am going away," he announced one day when I found him packing his old leather valises. "I may be gone all summer. I had this hand x-rayed in Lindsay and the verdict is that it was broken last winter and the bones haven't knit properly. I'm going to Rochester, Minnesota – to the Mayo Clinic – to have the thing seen to by specialists; probably have to have the hand re-broken. So – all this is going to require time.

"And you'll be in charge of the operation here. Sit down and we'll go over the business end of it together. We should have done this before now."

Mick laid out which cattle he wanted shipped and when, depending on the prevailing market conditions. He said he'd been losing money on cattle since the depression, beef prices being what they were; but Mick's notion of losing money meant that he wasn't making 100% profit. He showed me how to tally the record books, told me that the bank at Riverdale would give me whatever funds I needed, but that I wasn't to buy a new Marmon or overhaul the house by laying down Oriental carpets. He said if I needed help at any time with haying or whatever I could get old George Heeney or maybe Pat Marren from Slab Town.

"Anyway, I'll be in touch with you by letter. As soon as I get to the Mayo people I'll write and give you an address where you can send a telegram if the barn burns down or the house blows away. And look after Fenris – I've never been away for any length of time and it's just possible he may miss me. We're both getting old."

At first, I was too busy and too filled with the importance of running the shebang single-handed to get lonely. After a while, particularly in the evenings when the melt water was running free and the first red-wings were raising hell in the alder swamps, I began to miss my uncle. Once I took out his banjo and tried to strum something on it, but I wasn't cut out to be a musician. Besides, it seemed kind of irreverent to be fooling around with the thing when its owner was away and maybe never able to finger the strings himself again.

Elaine and I were writing two and three times a week now, and, when the Easter holidays began, I met her at Beaverton when she got off the train. If anything, she looked even prettier than I had remembered.

"Can we stop at Riverdale?" Elaine said when we were in the car. "I will have to arrange for a place to stay while I'm here."

I asked her what she meant by "a place to stay."

171

"Well Danny – I can't stay with you. What would the neighbours think?"

"Christ-all-Jesus! The only neighbour we have is George Heeney and he hasn't thought about anything for fifty years and not too much then. Look – if you're all worried about morals and a lot of stuff like that I can sleep outside; the weather's warming up and I sleep outside in good weather, anyhow. You can have Mick's bed – now that he isn't in it."

She laughed – that silvery fluting laugh that always made me think of blue-bells ringing or a hermit thrush deep in the piney woods calling to the evening star.

"All right, Danny. I'll feel perfectly moral and school-ma'amish for the whole stay. Just don't sleep too far away, though, in case I get frightened of things that go bump in the night. I will need your strong brown arm for protection."

"The only thing that bumped around in the night was Mick – or maybe Fenris."

"But aren't there ghosts? That old place must be alive with ghosts. What about old Kerwin Mulcahy – doesn't he come back and walk the creaking floors and chase his assortment of mistresses through the upstairs?"

I snorted. "Not very likely. Not even a ghost would trust a woman around that Mick."

"You're jealous of your uncle, aren't you?"

"I am *not!*"

She laughed delightedly. "Oh, but you are, Danny. It's one of those love-hate syndromes. I know – I studied all about it in psychology class at Western."

I changed the subject.

When we reached the road gate, I remembered that we were spang out of bread and milk and I drove on across the river to Horncastle. Elaine said she was thirsty, so she came into Rilance's with me. Naturally enough, half of Horncastle – the worst half – was inside and gawping as if they'd never seen a pretty girl in a short skirt before.

I went to the back of the store where the big wooden cooler was and got a bottle of Green River soda pop for Elaine. When I went to pay for the things I'd ordered, Doris Rilance said, "Seventy-five cents, please, and oh yes – five cents for the soft

172

drink. I'd rather thought you would be buying champagne – you know – to celebrate."

"This badger-hole isn't exactly a champagne town and yours isn't a champagne store. If you ran to wine I imagine it'd be Four Aces and not champagne. You're right about the celebration. I'd invite you except you couldn't be trusted around the butler."

Doris lifted her nose. "Oh, the Mulcahys have a butler, have they?"

"Yeah – George Heeney." I took Elaine's arm and piloted her out of the store. We were hardly down the steps when Charlie George's old woman and Doris got their heads together over the counter and began to buzz.

I put Elaine's luggage in Mick's room, which he seldom used. I was glad I had aired and swept it out, removing several generations of spider life from the closets. I even hung a pair of curtains across the window, and I went at the glass with Bon Ami and newspaper until it sparkled.

While Elaine was getting settled in, I saddled Gertie and went to see about a cow that was due to calf. I found her shacked up in the poplar grove against the 10th line. She was not only due, she had gone ahead and done it without any help from me – and twins at that. They looked kind of cute, with their little white faces and maroon bodies still dark and wet from being licked and groomed by the proud mother. They staggered around on spindly legs, bunting and blatting until they found a teat – one on each side.

By the time I got back to the house the dusk was setting in. Elaine had put an apron on over her dress and she was ankling around the kitchen in high-heeled pumps. The table was set and she'd made hot biscuits and an apple pie.

After supper, I fetched out a jar of Mick's white wheat whiskey, fixed Elaine's drink with hot water and vanilla and sugar the way she liked it, and we sat in the library. She examined the books, and while she was looking through an old leather-backed copy of Thoreau, a photo fell out. We looked at it. The photo was an ancient ambro-type of a girl in an old-fashioned dress with a choker collar; her hair was piled high on her head. She was a mighty pretty girl.

173

"Who is she?" Elaine asked.

I didn't know. I'd never seen that picture before.

Elaine turned it over. Across the back in a beautiful feminine hand was written: *To Michael with all my love.*

"I think we've just discovered a ghost," she said softly.

We talked deep into the night. Talked and drank. I was surprised at the amount of booze Elaine could put away; I was feeling the stuff and no mistake, but, except for being somewhat animated, Elaine gave no indication that she had been sipping generously at the powerful whiskey.

"Well." I began to feel sleepy. "I imagine you'll be tired after your trip. I'll just get my sleeping bag and stuff and say good-night."

She giggled. "Are you really going to sleep out on the cold, wet ground?"

"Those were the conditions, I thought."

"Oh sure – I forgot. The conditions." She giggled again.

"What's so damn funny?" I scowled.

"You're funny, Danny. Delightfully man-funny. Man-boy funny." She rose and put her arms around me.

"Kiss me good-night, funny Danny."

I kissed her and it was nohow like kissing your mother good-bye at the train station. Her little pointed tongue darted in and out of my mouth like a thing of fire. I pulled her close, feeling the swell of her breasts against my chest. She had kicked off her high heels; even so she was almost as tall as I was.

She burrowed her face against me. "Danny – go to bed. Go outside and go to bed." But she didn't make any move to get away.

I had a frog in my throat, or maybe it was a horny toad. At least I had trouble speaking.

"I guess maybe not. I guess the conditions have changed."

She moaned and settled herself even closer.

I went upstairs first; Elaine said she had things to do. Anyway, I was the bashful one, I suppose. I went up and got out of my clothes and got into bed and pulled the blankets up around my neck.

It seemed like a year that Elaine was down in the kitchen, splashing water around in an old china wash-bowl that had

174

pink china roses painted on the side. There was a jug that went with it – a big eary jug – but it was cracked down one side and leaked.

She came up the stairs in her stocking feet, carrying her shoes. She smiled and peeled off her dress and slip. It was the first time I'd ever seen a girl actually undress and my excitement was threatening to raise the blankets. She sat on the edge of the bed, unfastening, with terrible slowness, her garter-straps, ruefully examining a red mark high on her thigh where her stocking top had tightened.

When she had undressed, she turned around. My eyes rivetted on the wide swatch of dark, curling hair that made a big V between her legs. Her breasts jutted out firm and nipply.

She was in beside me and I took her in my arms and felt the smooth, creamy flesh of her next to me and smelled the good woman smell of her. I tried to settle myself on her, but she wriggled away and told me to wait. Her hands reached down and found me and did strange and terribly beautiful things to me – and to herself. When I could wait no longer, I thrust her down on the bed and the night rocked away all around us and we didn't even know it was there.

Afterward, we lay close to each other in the dark; her leg was across mine, possessively.

"The thought strikes me," I said, trying to talk like Uncle Mick, "that you didn't learn all that in teacher's college."

She didn't answer for a minute.

"No," she said gravely, "I didn't."

"Then where?" I was beginning to feel pretty jealous.

"Do you really want to know, Danny?"

"I asked you, didn't I?"

"Yes," she sighed, "you asked me. I learned it from men. I've been with men – you know that."

"How many men?" Now I was savage.

I heard her draw in her breath sharply. "Oh, I don't know – five – six. I suppose five or six."

"Well, for the love of dying Jesus! You don't know whether you've had five or six. . . ."

"I'm nineteen – going on twenty. I've been to college and I've taught in schools. Do you think me so unattractive that other men wouldn't be interested in me?" She sounded fierce.

I didn't say anything. I sulked in the darkness.

"How many times have you screwed Doris Rilance?" she asked quietly. I was surprised to hear her say "screwed."

"Well – once. Once was all."

"Did you like it? Was she good?"

I began to scout and barge a little. I wasn't going to take a back seat to Elaine's love affairs even if she was nineteen going on for twenty and had been to college.

"Oh, I've had worse," I remarked with a kind of forced off-handedness.

"But I'm better, aren't I?" She tightened her legs across me playfully.

"You're the best ever." I found her lips and kissed her.

Elaine made a pleased sound and snuggled her face into my shoulder. In a few minutes she was asleep and breathing softly against my arm.

I lay awake for a long time blinking at the ceiling I couldn't see. When I awoke Elaine was up and I could hear bacon frying down on the kitchen stove.

That evening Elaine looked out the east kitchen window and saw two men approaching by the lane under the elms.

"Look, Danny," she cried. "We have company."

"That's a loose description. It's George Heeney and Ed Rilance. I wonder what they want? Probably came over to snoop around and see what's been going on in the Mulcahy house of sin."

I think they did call out of pure curiosity, yet once they mumbled their embarrassed greetings to Elaine they fell right under her spell. She told George Heeney he looked as if he'd led a very interesting life and he blushed down to the neckline of his unlaundered wool underwear. If old Heeney's life had been interesting so was that of a fence lizard. Elaine won over Rilance by telling him that the country general store was the backbone of the nation and that dealing in one was such a pleasure after the impersonal service one got at the T. Eaton Company or Robert Simpson's. The storekeeper reared back with pleasure and struck into one of his long reminiscences.

176

"Yes, young lady, you've made a very shrewd observation there – very shrewd. Now you take me (I wondered who'd want him) – I been in business thirty-five years. My father before me had that store: Parker L. Rilance – you may have heard of him. He ran a good store."

"He was tighter'n a bull's arse in fly-time," offered Heeney. Rilance ignored that and rambulated on.

"Before my father it was Jones – Bartley Jones. You remember Bartley, George."

"No I don't and neither do you. He hung himself in that back part where you keep the hen feed; that was before I was born and I'm older'n you are. Hung himself with a piece of rope because his wife burned the pancakes."

"It wasn't a rope, it was fence wire," cackled Rilance triumphantly. "And it wasn't anything at all to do with pancakes – it was on account of she always fried his eggs sunny side up and he liked them once over lightly. Anyways, I mind when the hotel was still standing."

"What hotel?" I wanted to know.

"It was called the Moy House," said Rilance. "A fellow by the name of Horan run it for years. That was before my time. It used to stand just north of Charlie George's blacksmith shop. One of your people – Kerwin – used to get drunk in that hotel."

"Kerwin used to get drunk all over the country," put in George.

"After Horan left – up and moved to Delaware – that's down in the United States," he informed Elaine in case she didn't know, "a family named Sweeney moved in."

"I guess you could say they was a family," remarked Heeney. "Wa'nt nothin' but the old man and the two boys – Tommy and Rat."

"Rat? Why was he called Rat?" Elaine clapped her palm over her mouth in mirth, leaning back to show a fair amount of pretty leg above her stocking that I'd just as soon George Heeney hadn't been able to peer at.

"I dunno," he grunted, tearing his eyes away with so much effort you could almost hear them pull as they left. "He was called Rat as long as I mind. What was the old man's name, Ed? I don't recall ever hearing it."

"Pius. Named after one of them Popes, I guess."

"Anyways," Heeney continued, "they had a real boar's nest in that old hotel. They boarded up all but a couple of the rooms and they had about thirty fuck––, excuse me – they had a whole tribe of cats hanging around about half-fed and three-quarters starved. Well sir, one day Rat was over to Pecker Tow–– I mean, well he was over there someplace, drinkin' and he come home and he heard the fiddle goin' – Tommy used to scrape the fiddle now and again. So he goes in and there's the old man layin' dead on the kitchen floor – had a heart attack or somethin'. . . . ."

"A stroke," put in Rilance. "What they call one of them celestial hemorrhoids."

"Yeah, I guess that was it – anyways – the cats got at the corpse and was gnawin' hell out of it and Tommy fiddling away and paying no attention. Drunked up, I suppose. Later on Rat was tellin' some folks about it and he says, 'I get home and there's Tommy playin' "Hi-Jesus-Hoe-Her-Down-Christ" on the violin and the cats chewin' the face off father!' "

"Another time," Rilance took up the story, "Tommy bought a new pair of river-driving boots – both him and Rat used to work in the camps and drive the river. The next day Tommy was sick and couldn't go to work, so Rat swiped the new boots and damned if he didn't get drowned breaking a jam. Your grandfather got drowned in the same river and about the same place. Some of the boys went to Sweeney's and they says, 'Tommy, we got bad news – Rat got drowned in the river.' 'Holy bleeding ass-holes!' says Tommy, 'And him wearing me new boots!' "

George, having dropped his matches several times, the better to squint up Elaine's legs, took his turn.

"Rat and Tommy used to fight in the streets of Dog Town. They'd fight until they got all tuckered out and they'd lay side by side in the street and peg horse-shit at each other."

Having pretty well exhausted the subject of the Sweeneys, the pair of old blatherskites got up and moved toward the door. They said good-bye to Elaine, Rilance holding her hand so long and so tenderly I didn't know whether he was going to kiss it, bite it or take some of the fingers home to stick up on his mantelpiece for good luck charms. George Heeney ducked his head forward in what may have been intended for a bow, but his belly wouldn't let him follow through, so he bent one rheumatic leg and curtsied instead.

When they had flogged on up the trail, Elaine sat back in her chair and laughed so heartily I couldn't help but laugh with her.

I stood beside her and put my hand on the bare place where her stocking parted company with her leg, but she put her own hand down and clasped mine firmly.

"You behave yourself, to-night," she warned.

I wanted to know why.

"Well, let's just say it's that time of the month?"

"What time is that?"

She stared, then made out to laugh, then stopped.

"Danny – just how much do you know about women? Biologically, that is?"

I allowed as how I knew just about everything that was essential.

"Then you must know about menstruation."

"I don't know anything about that. What's administration got to do with it? With women, I mean?"

"Oh, you're funny. You're as big a Mrs. Malaprop as Ed Rilance."

"What in hell are you on about?"

"That's a character from Sheridan."

"I thought you'd heard enough about characters from Horncastle to last you through the summer. Where's Sheridan?"

She proceeded to tell me all about lunar cycles and menstrual changes and plays by Richard Sheridan. In the end I admitted I was as ignorant as a hog and as stupid as a burro.

"You might just as well quit teaching school and move in here for keeps and make me your star pupil," I declared. "It would be a full-time job."

She said she wished that were possible.

"Well, why can't you?"

"Danny! I have a father and mother."

"Hasn't everyone? No, I guess they don't. I don't."

She looked at me seriously. "You've never mentioned your parents to me. Where are they, Danny?"

"They're dead and buried." I looked away.

"Were you raised as an orphan – I mean before you came to live here with your uncle?"

"Nope."

"Don't you want to tell me?"

I told her.

She was quiet for a long time. "It just makes me want to love you all the more – to hold you and comfort you."

When we went to bed she held me in her arms all night.

The next time I picked up the mail, there was a letter from Uncle Mick. He had taken a room in that Rochester place and was having his hand seen to at the clinic there. He asked about Fenris and reminded me it was getting time to make the first shipment of beeves to Toronto. Then he took up the slack:

> Has Miss Warren visited as planned? If so, I hope you settled her in my old room; it has the only decent bed in the establishment. You, no doubt, are bunking down by the Perch, listening at night to the heady love-calls of the spring peepers and glorying in the scent of fresh cow droppings. Should Miss Warren be at all nervous, you might prevail on Fenris to take up his quarters with her at night. Give my love to Doris Rilance when next you date her. You have a splendid opportunity now that Miss Warren is there to take Doris to the movies. Miss Warren would, no doubt, be delighted to keep an eye on the stock during your absence. George Heeney could keep her company if she gets lonely.

> Be careful
> Michael Mulcahy.

FIFTEEN

Toward the end of Elaine's Easter vacation, a feeling of moroseness got a toe-hold inside me, sprouted and spread branches. I found myself missing her while she was still around. To think of Elaine being several hundred miles away, in touch only by letter, and maybe going out on dates with other men and maybe doing all of the same things with them she'd done with me, set my teeth on edge. I put up all manner of arguments to convince her she should stay – that we should get married – but she met them and parried each one with that baffling female logic that is all the more maddening because you know it makes sense.

"Danny," she pleaded, "try to understand my position. I've lied to my parents about where and how I was spending my

Easter vacation. They are – well – you would think of them as very stuffy and old-fashioned, but they have their principles and they believe in them. I'm their only child and it would distress them if I moved in here with you permanently. Daddy is a lawyer and has a certain amount of prestige in the community: belongs to the leading lodges and service organizations. Wrongly or rightly, they are proud of me and I just can't hurt them."

"We could get married and do the thing up respectable," I said stubbornly.

"That's just it," Elaine countered. "You're too young, Danny. I'm too young. You're still only sixteen, even if you do look and act ten years older."

"I'll be seventeen next month," I reminded her.

"All right, seventeen. But you still have a great deal of living to do, and while marriage and love and all that goes with it may look fine and wonderful to you now, you can't really say how you are going to feel about it a few years from now when you have a wife with curlers in her hair and babies crying in the middle of the night.

"You have a free, open style of living here with your uncle. Marriage means a curtailment of that freedom. You won't be able to saddle your horse and ride off over the pastures whenever you feel like it, with a wife and possibly children to demand so much of your time."

I stood at the kitchen window watching a grey spring drizzle pepper at the panes. I was beat and I knew it. An emptiness hollowed the pit of my stomach. The April dusk, spreading its wings through the poplars and filtering in across the green-brown hills was akin to the disappointment seeping bitterly through every fun-thought and good time I'd ever had.

Elaine was sewing a torn place in the sleeve of one of my shirts. She looked very girlish, yet somehow womanly and domestic, bent over her work, pins in her teeth.

"We'll wait five years," she planned. "Five years isn't long, Danny. Then we'll be married, have a glorious honeymoon and come back and live happily ever afterward in Brulé or wherever you want to live. That's how it must be."

"Yeah, sure," I said. "That's how it must be."

I got the whiskey and took a long, gut-shuddering belt of it. And another. And a third. Elaine watched me worriedly.

"Do be careful, Danny," she begged.

The liquor buzzed within me; it sent fire to my head.

"*Wahoo!*" I shouted. "I'm the last of the past and the bad Mulcahys!" I crashed my glass into the corner of the room.

"And why not! My mother was a whore and my old man a murderer and a suicide. Sure and by Jesus your folks wouldn't cotton to me and my style. Any maybe I just don't care a pinch of coon-shit one way or the other." I thrust my jaw out hard.

Elaine finished her sewing. She sat, staring at the checkered oilcloth on the table, saying nothing.

I grabbed my denim brush jacket off the hook, slid the whiskey flask down the front and wrenched out into the night rain. I had some idea of getting on the pony and riding off to hell and gone, or maybe taking the Plymouth and go ramming into Riverdale, or picking up Doris Rilance and banging her ass down some side-road.

Before I got it quite settled in my fuzzy brain precisely which shenanigan I honed to tie into, a string of car lights picked their way slowly down the muddy trail. I had some kind of a half-tipsy notion that it was a posse of police and Sunday-school superintendents gathered in force and by the regiment to come and arrest me for conduct prejudicial to the moral tone of the community. I balled my fists and grinned. A fight was just what I needed.

When the lead automobile unloaded, I could see that the occupants were hardly representative of the forces of law and order and public decency. Pat Marren came up, carefully warding the rain off his guitar with an oilskin slicker. Garnet Gifford was with him and Red John Burke and his wife, and a man and a woman I knew only as Tod and Leona Quill. The other cars spilled out Tom the Indian from Dog Town, and a couple of hefty squaws, and a thin Indian lad of about my age. And there came Tanglefoot carrying a whole gallon of sherry wine, and George Heeney and the two Healey brothers from West Mara, and a dozen or so mixed men and women I didn't know and had never heard of. Some were carrying musical instruments, mostly fiddles and guitars; some had cases of beer; others toted jugs that looked to contain homemade whiskey that was called mule-piss around Brulé.

They nodded or said "Evenin'," and hustled right by me and on into the house. This was the Brulé style of having a house party. They didn't warn you or wait for invitations. They came and they stayed and they danced and played and got drunk, and when they got tired they went home. When the last had filed inside, I followed after her; she was a mighty pretty girl with a crown of blondined hair around which she'd fixed a scarlet ribbon. She gave me an interested glance and giggled.

The Lord, I thought, giveth and the Lord taketh away. After the Lord had spent part of the evening taking, I was anxious to see what he was going to hand out during the remainder of the night.

Elaine corralled me as soon as I got inside.

"Danny, what on earth! Who are all these people and what do they want?"

I explained that they probably were set on having a shindig, Brulé fashion.

"Did you invite them?"

"Them?" I looked at Tanglefoot who, still holding her gallon of bingo, was treading the beginnings of a measure with George Heeney. "I wouldn't invite them to Semper Garrity's funeral. They invited themselves."

"But I look terrible," Elaine wailed. "This old dress . . . *ohhhhh!*"

"Go and dress for the party," I grinned. "It's like being hung. If you can't get out of it you might just as well enjoy the cart ride."

She turned and fled up the stairs.

The fiddlers scraped and squawked and tuned until they got their strings to the right pitch or close to it. Pat Marren ran his long, slender fingers speculatively across his guitar strings, looked sideways at the two violin players, nodded, and crying "Come on, George!" hit his guitar a lick, and the fiddlers swung into a fast jig.

I would never have thought old George Heeney had it in him. Sloppy big belly and all, he promenaded into the cleared

184

space in the centre of the kitchen and tapped his toes and heels like flickers of summer lightning in time to the music. He jigged through a chorus, then bawled out a ditty to the same tune.

Oh, a rich man lives in a big brick house –
Pore man lives in a frame;
But Jesse lives in the County Gaol
With a brick wall just the same.

The musicians stopped, eased their thirst a hair by guzzling beer straight from the bottle, then began again when Red John Burke yelled, "Partners for a square!"

The blonde girl with the good legs grabbed me by the arm and hauled me into the circle, although I'd never danced in my life and tried to tell her so.

"I'll push you through," she laughed, snugging her arm firmly around my waist. I felt needles tingling through me in the place where her arm was.

Choose your partners –
Your corners address –
Now all join hands –
Go 'way to the West –
Go 'way to the West!

Red John's delivery was loud if not intelligible. It was pure gibberish to me, not being accustomed to square-dancing or any other kind of dancing, for that matter. So whether Burke was calling a quadrille or the hogs for breakfast was all one with me. I knew the whiskey I'd drunk was running hot through my veins and that the blonde girl had a slender waist and awfully pretty knees that gave every indication that higher up was just as pretty and open to exploration.

At the grand finale when everybody swung their partners, I boosted mine out and twirled her around and about so that her legs trailed in the air and I did my level best to make out the colour of her panties, but I couldn't quite tell whether they were black or whether she wasn't wearing any and wasn't a real blonde all over.

185

At this point, Elaine came down the stairs, wearing a flame-coloured dress with tassels hung round the hem of the skirt and a deep V-bodice in front that showed a considerable chunk of bosom. She hadn't much more than enough time to glare at the blonde girl when George Heeney grabbed her, pulled her onto the floor and waltzed her around while roaring, to the tune of "My Bonny Lies Over the Ocean," his idea of a troubadour's ballad:

> My father's a drunken old bastard;
> My mother from scrubbing grows thin;
> My sister works nights in a cat-house;
> Good Christ! how the money rolls in.

There was another square-dance set which I sat out in the corner with the blonde girl on my knee and my hand squeezing her near breast. Elaine was partnered with one of the Healeys, the hem of her dress bouncing up and her alabaster thighs gleaming, as she romped gracefully through intricate dips and dives and chain manipulations.

After that, the crowd sat back to cool off and apply themselves to whatever booze they could lay their hands to. Tanglefoot, swaying to the side and also to the back and front, spooked herself alongside Pat Marren and warbled a song that consisted mostly of her being "In the Valley, *Yoo-Hoo.*" When she was finished yoo-hooing, the crowd politely abstained from laughing. One of the fiddlers, an accomplished player at that, dipped his bow and rolled out a long, singing, crooning wail on his violin that had a lot of blue-grass sound in it: full of train whistles and smoky hills and the sad call of wild birds at sundown. Pat Marren and a woman I didn't know sang in unison about an old drowning during a river drive. I remember a verse went:

> Come all of you bold shanty boys
> As I would have you see
> The green mound on the river bank
> Where grows the hemlock tree. . . .

186

Hearing that song made me feel twingey and kind of lonesome sad. I thought of Holly Dallan and her warm supple body floating down the cruel Black River until she was all drowned and pale and cold. The song must have affected George Heeney the same way because he came up to me with a bottle of beer in his hand and big tears glombing down his whiskery face.

"Oh, I remember the day your grandfather got it driving the river," he lamented. "That was one sad day for us all. We loaded him onto a wagon and old Kerwin. . . ."

"Come on, Danny-Boy," interrupted the blonde girl whose name, I learned, was Daisy. "Sing a song."

"Well I will," I flustered, "and Elaine can sing it with me."

I had in mind an old country air I'd learned long ago from my father, and on one of our walks together, when she was still teaching at the 10th School, I had run over the thing with Elaine. She had picked it up and sung a clear, sweet soprano to my own rough baritone which was not altogether unlike that of my uncle, only not as resonant yet.

Elaine was sitting with her feet curled beneath her over by the musicians. She was drinking beer. She blushed, but under prodding she came over, and after humming a note or two so that Pat Marren could catch the chord we began:

> One summer's day as I chanced to stray
> Down by Blackwater's side;
> It was in gazing all around me
> That an Irish girl I spied.
> All in the forepart of the day
> They rolled in sport and play;
> Then this young man arose and he put on his clothes,
> Saying, "Fare-thee-well today."
> "That was not the promise that you gave to me
> When you lay on my breast –
> You'd have made me believe with your lying tongue
> That the sun rose in the west."
> "Go home, go home, to your father's garden –
> Go home and cry your fill;
> You may think on the sad misfortune

I brought on with my wanton will."
"There is not a flower in this whole world
As easily led as I,
And when fishes can fly and the seas do run dry –
O 'tis then that you'll marry *I-I-Ighhhh*."

We got a great hand when that was finished, and the cheering made Elaine get all blushy and she beamed and stood happily with her hand in mine, although she remembered to whisper fiercely not to go making a fool of myself with that yellow-haired strumpet just because I'd had a few drinks and she wasn't always around to keep an eye on me.

Red John bellowed by God and didn't Danny-Boy sing just like Mick himself and didn't he wish old Mick was here to enjoy the party and if there was a tougher, harder man than Mick Mulcahy he'd like to see him, hadn't he all but destroyed Brad-Awl Callum and cleaned out the school board and him sixty-five if he was a minute.

Tanglefoot announced that she'd go to bed any time Mick Mulcahy asked her to, which caused George Heeney to remark, "Yeah, or up against a tree if he wanted, but don't keep a lamp burnin' while you're waitin' to be asked – you'll go through a lot of coal-oil that way."

Having caught their second wind, the dancers went at it again, the two Indian women prancing like a pair of pregnant burros through what they called "a shottees." I wasn't sure which one Indian Tom was married to, maybe both; anyway a fellow from East Mara by the name of Doolin was busy getting the dress of one of the squaws up to the vicinity of her belt buckle when Tom decided to assert his husbandly rights and pulled a knife. Red John Burke got a stranglehold on Indian Tom from behind and the young Indian lad belted Burke with a chair, while the remaining squaw, not wishing to be left out of things, sat on his face, which must have been worse than getting slugged with a kitchen chair. The other men piled in, either trying to stop the fight or keep it going. They pushed and cussed and hassled, and the girls screamed, and Tanglefoot solemnly poured the remainder of her jug of wine onto the head of one of the fiddlers and baptized him in the name of R. B. Bennett.

While the ruction was at the peak of its performance, Daisy cuddled up to me and begged prettily to be protected. Then she wanted to know in which direction the toilet lay, and she indicated that I might as well come along and show her where it was and also protect her further from whatever might be out there from which she needed protecting. We were on our way when I heard my name called. I hadn't realized that Elaine could get that loud.

"You can find your way to the bathroom quite well by yourself, dear," Elaine said, smiling like a tiger.

The blonde had drunk a bit more than was good for her. "Bathroom?" she blinked. "I wasn't going to take a bath."

"I know," Elaine replied. "Not that you don't need it. Straight out the back door. You can't miss it. Not that it would matter to you if you did. Danny – perhaps you had better find the mop; I think Tanglefoot has had an accident."

That she had, all over the floor. She was sitting in it, making circles in it with one finger.

It required the best part of an hour to get rid of the last of them and get the place cleaned up. The kitchen looked as if a freight train had got derailed in it. We sprinkled cresol all around to dampen the smell of Tanglefoot. Before staggering out, Heeney got hold of Elaine and tried to plant a bearded kiss on her face which she ducked enough so that he merely spit in her ear.

When we were finished, I lifted Elaine in my arms and carried her upstairs, panting a little more than I would have liked; she was heavier that she looked. I flopped her on the bed and myself on top of her, although she kicked and squealed and threatened to scream rape.

"You make nice raping," I teased, afterward.

"Danny," she said softly.

"Yeah?"

"Danny – can we wait five years? Do I dare trust you that long around these predatory Brulé blondes?

"We'll just have to wait," she continued. "There's no other way. I'll go back to Petrolia and write to my parents . . . I'll write to you – every day, and. . . ."

The rest of what she was going to say got lost because I put my mouth hard against hers while a killdeer outside the window cried all the way across the pasture just streaking with the first light of dawn.